AF306751

Defoe Abbott Marx Hardy Melville Montaigne Machiavelli Chesterton Cooper Emerson Joyce Austen Hugo Eliot Grimm Molière Haggard Carroll Christie Maupassant Byron Schiller Stoker Wilde Engels Garnett Goethe Einstein Fitzgerald Hawthorne Smith Kafka Dostoyevsky Hall Cotton Kipling Doyle Willis Baum Henry Nietzsche Balzac Leslie Dumas Flaubert Turgenev Crane Stockton Vatsyayana Verne Burroughs Vinci Curtis Tocqueville Gogol Busch Homer Widger Tolstoy Whitman Darwin Thoreau Twain Scott Potter Freud Zola Lawrence Plato Harte Kant Jowett Stevenson Dickens Hesse Andersen Burton London Descartes Cervantes Poe Aristotle Wells Voltaire Cooke Hale James Hastings Bunner Shakespeare Irving Richter Chambers da Shaw Wodehouse Alcott Doré Dante Chekhov Pushkin Swift Newton Benedict

 tredition®



## Project Gutenberg

# Reason and Faith, Their Claims and Conflicts From The Edinburgh Review, October 1849, Volume 90, No. CLXXXII. (Pages 293-356)

Henry Rogers

# Imprint

This book is part of TREDITION CLASSICS

Author: Henry Rogers
Cover design: Buchgut, Berlin – Germany

Publisher: tredition GmbH, Hamburg - Germany
ISBN: 978-3-8424-7872-5

www.tredition.com
www.tredition.de

# REASON AND FAITH; THEIR CLAIMS AND CONFLICTS.

[by Henry Rogers]

**THE EDINBURGH REVIEW,**

**OCTOBER, 1849.**

[Volume 90] No. CLXXXII. [Pages 293-356]

Art.I—1. Historic Doubts relative to Napoleon Buonaparte Eighth edition, pp. 60. 8vo. London. 2. The Nemesis of Faith. By J. A. Froude,
M. A., Fellow of Exeter College, Oxford. 12mo. London: pp. 227. 3. Popular Christianity, its Transition State and Probable Development. By
F. J. Foxton, B. A.; formerly of Pembroke College, Oxford, and Perpetual
Curate of Stoke Prior and Docklow, Herefordshire. 12mo. London: pp. 226.

'Reason and Faith,' says one of our old divines, with the quaintness characteristic of his day, 'resemble the two sons of the patriarch; Reason is the firstborn, but Faith inherits the blessing. The image is ingenious, and the antithesis striking; but nevertheless the sentiment is far from just. It is hardly right to represent Faith as younger than reason: the fact undoubtedly being, that human creatures trust and believe, long before they reason or know. But the truth is, that both reason and Faith are coeval with the nature of man, and were designed to dwell in his heart together. In truth they are, and were, and, in such creatures as ourselves, must be, reciprocally complementary—neither can exclude the other. It is as impossible to exercise an acceptable faith without reason for so exercising it,—that is, without exercising reason while we exercise faith*,—as it is to apprehend by our reason, exclusive of faith, all the truths on which we are daily compelled to act, whether in relation to this world or the next. Neither is it right to represent either of them as failing of the promised heritage, except as both may fail alike, by perversion from their true end, and depravation of their genuine nature; for it to the faith of which the New Testament speaks so much, a peculiar blessing is promised, it is evident from the same volume that it is not a 'faith without reason' any more than a 'faith without works,' which is approved by the Author of Christianity. And this is sufficiently proved by the injunction 'to be ready to give a reason for the hope,'—and therefore for the faith,—'which is in us.'

———

* Let it be said that we are here playing upon an ambiguity in the word Reason;—considered in the first clause as an argument; and in the second, as the characteristic endowment of our species. The distinction between Reason and Reasoning (though most important) does not affect our statement; for though Reason may be exercised where there is no giving of reasons, there can be no giving of reasons without the exercise of Reason.

———

If, therefore, we were to imitate the quaintness of the old divine, on whose dictum we have been commenting, we should rather compare Reason and Faith to the two trusty spies, 'faithful amongst the 'faithless,' who confirmed each other's report of 'that good land which flowed with milk and honey,' and to both of whom the promise of a rich inheritance there was given,—and, in due time, amply redeemed. Or, rather, if we might be permitted to pursue the same vein a little further, and throw over our shoulders for a moment that mantle of allegory which none but Bunyan could wear long and successfully, we should represent Reason and Faith as twinborn beings,—the one, in form and features the image of manly beauty,—the other, of feminine grace and gentleness; but to each of whom, alas! was allotted a sad privation. While the bright eyes of Reason are full of piercing and restless intelligence, his ear is closed to sound; and while Faith has an ear of exquisite delicacy, on her sightless orbs, as she lifts them towards heaven, the sunbeam plays in vain. Hand in hand the brother and sister, in all mutual love, pursue their way, through a world on which, like ours, day breaks and night falls alternate; by day the eyes of Reason are the guide of Faith, and by night the ear of Faith is the guide of Reason. As is wont with those who labour under these privations respectively Reason is apt to be eager, impetuous, impatient of that instruction which his infirmity will not permit him readily to apprehend; while Faith, gentle and docile, is ever willing to listen to the voice by which alone truth and wisdom can effectually reach her.

It has been shown by Butler in the fourth and fifth chapters (Part I.) of his great work, that the entire constitution and condition of man, viewed in relation to the present world alone, and consequently all the analogies derived from that fact in relation to a future world, suggest the conclusion that we are here the subjects of a probation discipline, or in a course of education for another state of existence. But it has not, perhaps, been sufficiently insisted on, that if in the actual course of that education, of which enlightened obedience to the 'law of virtue,' as Butler expresses it, or, which is the same thing, to the dictates of supreme wisdom and goodness, is the great end, we give an unchecked ascendency to either Reason or Faith, we vitiate the whole process. The chief instrument by which that process is carried on is not Reason alone, or Faith alone, but their well-balanced and reciprocal interaction. It is a system of alternate checks and limitations, in which Reason does not supersede Faith, nor Faith encroach on Reason. But our meaning will be more evident when we have made one or two remarks on what are conceived to be their respective provinces. In the domain of Reason men generally include, 1st, what are called 'intuitions,' 2d, 'necessary deductions' from them; and 3d, deductions from their own direct 'experience; while in the domain of Faith are ranked all truths and propositions which are received, not without reasons indeed, but for reasons underived from the intrinsic evidence (whether intuitive or deductive, or from our own experience) of propositions themselves;—for reasons (such as credible testimony, for example,) extrinsic to the proper meaning and significance of such propositions: although such reasons, by accumulation and convergency, may be capable of subduing the force of any difficulties or improbabilities, which cannot be demonstrated to involve absolute contradictions.*

———

* Of the first kind of truths, or those received by intuition, we have examples in what are called 'self-evident axioms,' and 'fundamental laws' or 'conditions of thought,' which no wise man has ever attempted to prove. Of the second, we have examples in the whole fabric of mathematical science, reared from its basis of axioms and definitions, as well as in every other necessary deduction from admitted premises. The third virtually includes any conclusion in science based on direct experiment, or observation; though the belief of the truth even of Newton's system of the world, when received as Locke says he received and as the generality of men receive it, — without being able to follow the steps by which the great geometer proves his conclusions, — may be represented rather as an act of faith rather than an act of Reason; as much so as a belief in the truth of Christianity, founded on its historic and other evidences. The greater part of man's knowledge, indeed, even of science, — even the greater part of a scientific man's knowledge of science, based as it is on testimony alone (and which so often compels him to renounce to-day what he thought certain yesterday), — may be not unjustly considered as more allied to Faith than Reason. It may be said, perhaps, that the above classification of the truths received by Reason and Faith respectively is arbitrary; that even as to some of their alleged sources, they are not always clearly distinguishable; that the evidence of experience may in some sort be reduced to testimony, — that of sense, and testimony reduced to experience, — that of human veracity under given circumstances; both being founded upon the observed uniformity of certain phenomena under similar conditions. We admit the truth of this; and we admit it the more willingly, as it shows that so inextricably intertwined are the roots both of Reason and Faith in our nature, that no definitions that can be framed will completely separate them; none that will not involve many phenomena which may be said to fall under the dominion of one as much as the other. We have been content, for our practical purpose, without any too subtle refinement, to take the line of demarcation which is, perhaps, as obvious as any, and as

generally recognised. Few would say that a generalised inference from direct experience was not matter of reason rather than of faith; though an act of faith is involved in the process; and few would not call confidence in testimony where probabilities were nearly balanced, by the name of faith rather than reason, though an act of reason is involved in that process. We are much more anxious to show their general involution with one another than the points of discrimination between them. ____

In receiving important doctrines on the strength of such evidence, and in holding to them against the perplexities they involve, or, what is harder still, against the prejudices they oppose, every exercise of an intelligent faith will, on analysis, be found to consist; its only necessary limit will be proven contradictions in the propositions submitted to it; for, then, no evidence can justify belief, or even render it possible. But no other difficulties, however, great, will justify unbelief, where man has all that he can justly demand, — evidence such in its nature as he can deal with, and on which he is accustomed to act in his most important affairs in this world (thus admitting its validity), and such in amount as to render it more likely that the doctrines it substantiates are true, than, from mere ignorance of the mode in which these difficulties can be solved, he can infer them to be false. 'Probabilities,' says Bishop Bulter, 'are to us the very guide to life; and when the probabilities arise out of evidence which we are competent to pronounce, and the improbabilities merely from our surmises, where we have no evidence to deal with, and perhaps, from the limitation of our capacities, could not deal with it, if we had it, it is not difficult to see what course practical wisdom tells man he ought to pursue; and which he always does pursue, whatever difficulties beset him, — in all cases except one!

Such is the strict union — that mutual dependence of Reason and Faith — which would seem to be the great law under which the moral school in which we are being educated is conducted. This law is equally, or almost equally, its characteristic, Whether we regard man simply in his present condition, or in his present in relation to his future condition, — as an inhabitant only of this world, or a can-

didate for another; and to this law, by a series of analogies as striking as any of those which Butler has pointed out (and on which we
heartily wish his comprehensive genius had expended a chapter or
two), Christianity, in the demands it makes on both principles con-
jointly, is evidently adapted.

Men often speak, indeed, as if the exercise of faith was excluded
from their condition as inhabitants of the present world. But it requires but a very slight consideration to show that the boasted pre-
rogative of reason is here also that of a limited monarch; and that its
attempts to make itself absolute can only end in its own dethrone-
ment, and, after successive revolutions, in all the anarchy of absolute pyrrhonism.

For in the intellectual and moral education of man, considered
merely as a citizen of the present world, we see the constant and
inseparable union of the two principles, and provision made for
their perpetual exercise. He cannot advance a step, indeed without
both. We see faith demanded not only amidst the dependence and
ignorance in which childhood and youth are passed; not only in the
whole process by which we acquire the imperfect knowledge which
is to fit us for being men; but to the very last we may be truly said to
believe far more than we know. 'Indeed,' said Butler, 'the unsatisfac-
tory nature of the evidence with which we are obliged to take up in
the daily course of life, is scarce to be expected.' Nay, in an intelligible sense, even the 'primary truths,' or 'first principles,' or 'fundamental laws of thought,' or 'self-evident maxims,' or 'intuitions,' or
by whatever other names philosophers have been pleased to desig-
nate them, which, in a special sense, are the very province of reason,
as contra-distinguished from 'reasoning' or logical deduction, may
be said almost as truly to depend on faith as on reason for their
reception.* For the only ground for believing them true is that man
cannot help so believing them! The same may be said of that great
fact, without which the whole world would be at a stand-still — a
belief in the uniformity of the phenomena of external nature; that
the same sun, for example, which rose yesterday and to-day, will
rise again tomorrow. That this cannot be demonstrated, is admitted
on all hands; and that it is not absolutely proved from experience is
evident, both from the fact that the uniformity supposed is only
accepted as partially and transiently true; the great bulk of man-

kind, even while they so confidently act upon that uniformity, rejecting the idea of its being an eternal uniformity. Every theist believes that the order of the universe once began to be; and every Christian and most other men, believe that it will also one day cease to be.

------

* Common language seems to indicate this: Since we call that disposition of mind which leads some men to deny the above fundamental truths (or affect to deny them), not by a word which indicates the opposite of reason, but the opposite of faith, — Scepticism, Unbelief, Incredulity. ____

But perhaps the most striking example of the helplessness to which man is soon reduced if he relies upon his reason alone, is The spectacle of the issue of his investigations into that which one would imagine he must know most intimately, if he knows anything; and that is, his own nature — his own mind. There is something, to one who reflects long enough upon it, inexpressibly whimsical in the questions which the mind is for ever putting to itself respecting itself; and to which the said mind returns from its dark caverns only an echo. We are apt, when we speculate about the mind, to forget for the moment, that it is at once the querist and the oracle: and to regard it as something out of itself, like a mineral in the hands of the analytic chemist. We cannot fully enter into the absurdities of its condition, except by remembering that it is our own wise selves who so grotesquely bewilder us. The mind, on such occasions, takes itself (if we may so speak) into its own hands, turns itself about itself, listens to the echo of its own voice, and is obliged, after all, to lay itself down again with a very puzzled expression — and acknowledge that of its very self, itself knows little or nothing! 'I am material,' exclaims one of those whimsical beings, to whom the heaven-descended 'Know thyself' would seem to have been ironically addressed. 'No! — immaterial,' says another. 'I am both material and immaterial,' exclaims, perhaps, the very same mind at different times. 'Thought itself may be matter modified,' says one. 'Rather,' says another of the same perplexed species, 'matter is thought modified; for what you call matter is but a phenomenon.' But are independent and totally distinct substances, mysteriously, inexplicably conjoined,' says a third. 'How they are conjoined we know no more than the dead. Not so much, perhaps.' 'Do I ever cease to think,' says the mind to itself, 'even in sleep? Is not my essence thought?' 'You ought to know your own essence best,' all creation will reply. 'I am confident,' says one, 'that I never do cease to think,—not even in the soundest sleep.' 'You do, for a long time, every night of your life,' exclaims another, equally confident and equally ignorant. 'Where do I exist?' it goes on. 'Am I in the brain? Am I in the whole body? 'Am I anywhere? Am I nowhere?' 'I cannot have any local existence, for I know I am immaterial,' says one. 'I have a local existence, because I am material,' says another. 'I have a local existence, though I am not material,' says a third. 'Are my habitual actions voluntary,' it exclaims, 'however rapid they become; though I am unconscious of these volitions when they have attained a certain rapidity; or do I become a mere automaton as respects such actions? and therefore an automaton nine times out of ten, when I act at all?' To this query two opposite answers are given by different minds; and by others, perhaps wiser, none at all; while, often, opposite answers are given by the same mind at different times. In like manner has every action, every operation, every emotion of the mind been made the subject of endless doubt and disputation. Surely if, as Soame Jenyns imagined, the infirmities of man, and even graver evils, were permitted in order to afford amusement to superior intelligences, and make the angels laugh, few things could afford them better sport than the perplexities of this child of clay engaged in the study of himself. 'Alas,' exclaims at last the baffled spirit of this babe in intellect, as he surveys his shattered toys—his broken theories of metaphysics, 'I know that I am; but what I am—where I am—even how I act—not only what is my essence, but what even my mode of operation,—of all this I know nothing; and, boast of reason as I may, all that I think on these points is matter of opinion—or is matter of faith!' He resembles, in fact, nothing so much as a kitten first introduced to its own image in a mirror: she runs to the back of it, she leaps over it, she turns and twists, and jumps and frisks, in all directions, in the vain attempt to reach the fair illusion; and, at length, turns away in weariness from that incomprehensible enigma—the image of herself.

One would imagine—perhaps not untruly—that the Divine Creator had subjected us to these difficulties—and especially that incomprehensible trilemma,—that there is an union and interaction of two totally distinct substances, or that matter is but thought, or that thought is but matter,—one of which must be true, and all of which approach as near to the mutual contradictions as can well be conceived,—for the very purpose of rebuking the presumption of man, and of teaching him humility; that He had left these obscurities at the very threshold—nay, within the very mansion of the mind itself,—for the express purpose of deterring man from playing the dogmatising fool when he looked abroad. Yet, in spite of his raggedness and poverty at home, no sooner does man look out of his dusky dwelling, than, like Goldsmith's little Beau, who, in his garret up five pair of stairs, boasts of his friendship with lords, he is apt to assume airs of magnificence, and, glancing at the infinite through his little eye-glass, to affect an intimate acquaintance with the most respectable secrets of the universe!

It is undeniable, then, that the perplexities which uniformly puzzle man in the physical world, and even in the little world of his own mind, when he passes a certain limit, are just as unmanageable as those found in the moral constitution and government of the universe, or in the disclosures of the volume Revelation. In both we find abundance of inexplicable difficulties sometimes arising from our absolute ignorance, and perhaps quite as often from our partial knowledge. These difficulties are probably left on the pages of both volumes for some of the same reasons; many of them, it may be, because even the commentary of the Creator himself could not render them plain to finite understanding, though a necessary and salutary exercise of our humility may be involved in their reception; others, if not purely (which seems not probable) yet partly for the sake of exercising and training that humility, as an essential part of the education of a child; others, surmountable, indeed, in the progress of knowledge and by prolonged effort of the human intellect, may be designed to stimulate that intellect to strenuous action and healthy effort—as well as to supply, in their solution, as time rolls on, an ever-accumulating mass of proofs of the profundity of the wisdom which has so far anticipated all the wisdom of man; and of the divine origin of both the great books which he is privileged to study as a pupil, and even to illustrate as a commentator, — but the text of which he cannot alter.

But, for submitting to us many profound and insoluble problems, the second of the above reasons — the training of the intellect and heart of man to submission to the Supreme Intelligence alone be sufficient. For it; as is indicated by every thing in human nature, and by the representations of Scripture, which are in analogy with both, the present world is but the school of man in this the childhood of his being, to prepare him for the enjoyment of an immortal manhood in another, everything might be expected to be subordinated to this great end; and as the end of that education, can be no other than an enlightened obedience to God, the harmonious and concurrent exercise of reason and faith becomes absolutely necessary — not of reason to the exclusion of faith, for otherwise there would be no adequate test of man's docility and submission; nor of a faith that would assert itself, not only independent of reason, but in contradiction to it, — which would not be what God requires, and what alone can quadrate with that intelligent nature He has impressed on His offspring — a reasonable obedience. Implicit obedience, then, to the dictates of an all-perfect wisdom, exercised amidst many difficulties and perplexities, as so many tests of sincerity, and yet sustained by evidences which justify the conclusions which involve them, would seem to be the great object of man's moral education here; and to justify both the partial evidence addressed to his reason, and the abundant difficulties which it leaves to his faith. 'The evidence of religion,' says Butler, 'is fully sufficient for all the purposes of probation, how far soever it is from being satisfactory as to the purposes of curiosity, or any other: and, indeed, it answers the purposes of the former in several respects which it would not do if it were as over-bearing as is required.'* Or as Pascal beautifully puts it: — 'There is light enough for those whose sincere wish is to see, — and darkness enough to confound those of an opposite disposition.'+

------

* Analogy, part 2. chap. viii. + Pensees. Faugere's edition, tom. ii. p. 151. The views here developed will be found an expansion of some brief hints at the close of the article on Pascal's 'Life and Ge-

nius' (Ed. Review, Jan. 1847), though our space then prevented us from more than touching these topics. We may add that we gladly take this opportunity of pointing the attention of our readers to a tract of Archbishop Whately's, entitled 'The example of children as proposed to Christians,' which his Grace, having been struck with a coincidence between some of the thoughts in the tract and those expressed in the 'Review,' did us the favour to transmit to us. Had we seen the tract before, we should have been glad to illustrate and confirm our own views by those of this highly gifted prelate. We earnestly recommend the tract in question (as well as the whole of the remarkable volume in which it is now incorporated, 'Essays on some of the Peculiarities of the Christian Religion') to the perusal of our readers, and at the same time venture to express our conviction (having been led by the circumstances above mentioned to a fuller acquaintance with his Grace's theological writings than we had previously possessed) that, though this lucid and eloquent writer may, for obvious reasons, be most widely known by his 'Logic and 'Rhetoric,' the time will come when his Theological works will be, if not more widely read, still more highly prized. To great powers of argument and illustration, and delightful transparency of diction and style, he adds a higher quality still—and a very rare quality it is—an evident and intense honesty of purpose, an absorbing desire to arrive at the exact truth, and to state it with perfect fairness and with the just limitations. Without pretending to agree with all that Archbishop Whately has written on the subject of theology (though be carries his readers with him as frequently as any writer with whom we are acquainted) we may remark that in relation to that whole class of subjects, to which the present essay has reference, we know of no writer of the present day whose contributions are more numerous or more valuable. The highly ingenious ironical brochure, entitled 'Historic Doubts relative to Napoleon Buonaparte;' the Essays above mentioned, 'On some of the Peculiarities of the Christian Religion;' those 'On some of the Dangers to Christian Faith,' and on the 'Errors of Romanism;' the work on the 'Kingdom of Christ,' not to mention others, are well worthy of universal perusal. They abound in views both original and just, stated with all the author's aptness of illustration and transparency of language. We may remark, too, that in many of his occasional sermons, he has incidentally added many most beautiful fragments to that ever ac-

cumulating mass of internal evidence which the Scriptures themselves supply in their very structure, and which is evolved by diligent investigation of the relation and coherence of one part of them
with another. We are also rejoiced to see that a small and unpre-
tending, but very powerful, little tract, by the same writer, entitled
'Introductory Lessons on Christian Evidences.' has passed through
many editions, has been translated into most of the European languages, and, amongst the rest, very recently into German, with an
appropriate preface, by professor Abeltzhauser, of the University of
Dublin. It shows to demonstration that as much of the evidence of
Christianity as is necessary for conviction may be made perfectly
clear to the meanest capacity' and that, in spite of the assertions of
Rome and of Oxford to the contrary, the apostolic injunction to
every Christian to be ready to render a reason 'for the hope that is in
him,'—somewhat better than that no reason of the Hindoo or the
Hottentot, that he believes what he is told, without any reason except that he is told it,—is an injunction possible to obey. _____

As He 'who spake as never man spake' is pleased often to illustrate the conduct of the Father of Spirits to his intelligent offspring
by a reference to the conduct which flows from the relations of the
human parent to his children, so the present subject admits of similar illustration. What God does with us in that process of moral
education to which we have just adverted, is exactly what every
wise parent endeavours to do with his children,—though by methods, as we may well judge, proportionably less perfect. Man too
instinctively, or by reflection, adapts himself to the nature of his
children; and seeing that only so far as it is justly trained can they be
happy, makes the harmonious and concurrent development of their
reason and their faith his object; he too endeavours to teach them
that without which they cannot be happy,—obedience, but a reasonable obedience He gives them, in his general procedure and
conduct, sufficient proof of his superior knowledge, superior wisdom, and unchanging love; and secure in the general effect of this,
he leaves them to receive by faith many things which he cannot
explain to them if he would, till they get older; many things which
he can only partially explain; and others which he might more perfectly explain, but will not, partly as a test of their docility and partly to invite and necessitate the healthy and energetic exercise of

their reason in finding out the explanation for themselves. Confiding in the same general effect of his procedure and conduct, he does not hesitate, when the foresight of their ultimate welfare justifies it, to draw still more largely on their faith, in acts of apparent harshness and severity. Time, he knows, will show, though perhaps not till his yearning heart has ceased to beat for their welfare, that all that all he did, he did in love. He knows, too, that if his lessons are taken aright, and his children become the good and happy men he wishes them to be, they will say, as they visit his sepulchre, and recall with sorrow the once unappreciated love which animated him, — and perhaps with a sorrow, deeper still, remember the transient resentments caused by a solitary severity: 'He was indeed a friend; he corrected us not for his pleasure, but for our profit; and what we once thought was caprice or passion, we now know was love.'

These analogies afford a true, though most imperfect, representation of the moral discipline to which Supreme Wisdom is subjecting us; and as we are accustomed to despair of any child with whom parental experience and authority go for nothing, unless he can fully understand the intrinsic reasons for every special act of duty which that experience and authority dictate; as we are sure that he who has not learned to obey when young will never, when of age, know how to govern either himself or others: so a singular conduct in all the children of dust towards the Father of Spirits justifies a still more gloomy augury; inasmuch as the difference between the knowledge of man and the ignorance of a child, absolutely vanishes, in comparison with that interval which must ever subsist between the knowledge of the Eternal and the ignorance of man.

The remarks that have been made are not uncalled for in the present day. For unfortunately, it is now easy to detect in many classes of minds a tendency to divorce Reason from Faith, or Faith from reason; and to proclaim that 'what God hath joined together' shall henceforth exist in alienation. We see this tendency manifested in relation both to Natural Theology, and to Revealed Religion. The old conflict between the claims of these two guiding principles of man (in no age wholly suppressed) is visibly renewed in our day. In relation to Christianity especially, there are large classes amongst us who press the claims of faith so far, that it would become, if they had their will, an utterly unreasonable faith; some of whom do not scruple to speak slightingly of the evidences which substantiate Christianity; to decry and depreciate the study of them; to pronounce that study unnecessary; and even in many cases to insinuate their insufficiency. They are loud in the mean time in extolling a faith which, as Whately truly observes, is no whit better than the faith of a heathen; who has no other or better reason to offer for his religion than that his father told him it was true! But this plainly is not the intelligent faith which, as we have seen, is everywhere inculcated and applauded in the Scriptures; it is not 'that faith by which Christianity, appealing In the midst of a multitude of such traditional religions, to palpable evidence addressed to man's senses and understandings (in a way no other religion ever did) everywhere destroyed the systems for which their votaries could only say that their fathers told them they were true. And yet this blind belief in such tradition, many advocates of Christianity would now enjoin us to imitate! It might have occurred to them, one would think, that, on their principles, Christianity never could have succeeded; for every mind must have been hopelessly pre-occupied against all examination of its claims. It is, indeed, incomparably better that a man should be a sincere Christian even by an utterly unreasoning and passive faith (if that be possible), than no Christian at all; but at the best, such a man is a possessor of the truth only by accident: he ought to have, and, if he be a sincere disciple of truth, will seek, some more solid grounds for holding it. But it is but too obvious, we fear, that the disposition to enjoin this obsequious mood of mind is prompted by a strong desire to revive the ancient empire of priestcraft and the pretensions of ecclesiastical despotism; to secure readmission to the human mind of extravagant and preposterous claims, which their advocates are sadly conscious rest on no solid foundation. They feel that reason is not with them, it must be against them: and reason therefore they are determined to exclude.

But the experience of the present 'developments' of Oxford teaching may serve to show us how infinitely perilous is this course; and how fearfully, both outraged reason and outraged faith will avenge the wrongs done them by their alienation and disjunction. Those results, indeed, we predicted in 1843; before a single leader of the Oxford school had gone over to Rome, and before any tendencies to the opposite extreme of Scepticism had manifested themselves. We then affirmed that, on the one hand, those who were contending for the corruptions of the fourth century could not possibly find footing there, but must inevitably seek their ultimate resting place in Rome—a prediction which has been too amply fulfilled; and that, on the other, the extravagant pretensions put forth on behalf of an uninquiring faith, and the desperate assertion that the 'evidence for Christianity' was no stronger than that for 'Church Principles,' must, by reaction, lead on to an outbreak of infidelity. That prophecy, too, has been to the letter accomplished. We then said,—

"We have seen it recently asserted by some of the Oxford school that there is as much reason for rejecting the most essential doctrines of Christianity—nay Christianity itself—as for rejecting their "church principles." That, in short, we have as much reason for being infidels as for rejecting the doctrine of Apostolical succession! What other effect such reasoning can have than that of compelling men to believe that there is nothing between infidelity and popery, and of urging them to make a selection between the two, we know not …. Indeed, we fully expect that, as a reaction of the present extravagancies, of the revival of obsolete superstition, we shall have ere long to fight over again the battle with a modified form of infidelity, as now with a modified form of popery. Thus, probably, for some time to come, will the human mind continue to oscillate between the extremes of error; but with a diminished are at each vibration; until truth shall at last prevail, and compel it to repose in the centre."*

————

* Oxford Tract School, Ed. Rev., April, 1843. ____


The offensive displays of self-sufficiency and flippancy, of ignorance and presumption, found in the productions of the apostles of the new infidelity of Oxford, (of which we shall have a few words to say by-and-by) are the natural and instructive, though most painful, result of attempting to give predominance to one principle of our nature, where two or more are designed reciprocally to guard and check each other; and such results must ever follow such attempts.

The excellence of man—so complexly constituted is his nature—must consist in the harmonious action and proper balance of all the constituents of that nature; the equilibrium he sighs for must be the result of the combined action of forces operating in different directions; of his reason, his faith, his appetites, his affections, his emotions; when these operate each in due proportion, then, and then only, can he be at rest. It may, indeed, transcend any calculus of man to estimate exactly the several elements in this complicated polygon of forces; but we are at least sure that, if any one principle be so developed as to supersede another, no safe equipoise will be attained. We all know familiarly enough that this is the case when the affections or the appetites are more powerful than the reason and the conscience, instead of being in subjection to them: but it is not less the case, though the result is not so palpable, when reason and faith either exclude one another, or trench on each other's domain; when one is pampered and the other starved.* Hence the perils attendant upon their attempted separation, and the ruin which results from their actual alienation and hostility. There is no depth of dreary superstition into which men may not sink in the one case, and no extravagance of ignorant presumption to which they may not soar in the other. It is only by the mutual and alternate action of these different forces that man can safely navigate his little bark through the narrow straits and by the dangerous rocks which impede his course; and if Faith spread not the sail to the breeze, or if Reason desert the helm, we are in equal peril. _____

* It has been our lot to meet with disciples of the Oxford Tract School, who have, by a fatal indulgence of an appetite of belief; brought themselves to believe any mediaeval miracle, nay, any ghost story, without examination, saying, with a solemn face, 'It is better to believe that to reason.' They believe as they will to believe; and thus is reason avenged. Reason, similarly indulged, believes, with Mr. Foxton and Mr. Froude, that a miracle is even an impossibility; and this is the 'Nemesis' of faith. _____

If it be said that this is a disconsolate and dreary doctrine; that man seeks and needs a simpler navigation than this troublesome and intricate course, by star and chart, compass and lead line; and that this responsibility, of ever

'Sounding on his dim and perilous way,'

is too grave for so feeble a nature; we answer that such is his actual condition. This is a plain matter of fact which cannot be denied. The various principles of his constitution, and his position in relation to the external world, obviously and absolutely subject him to this very responsibility throughout his whole course in this life. It is never remitted or abated: resolves are necessitated upon imperfect evidence; and action imperatively demanded amidst doubts and difficulties in which reason is not satisfied, and faith is required. To argue therefore, that God cannot have left man to such uncertainty, is to argue, as the pertinacious lawyer did, who, on seeing a man in the stocks, asked him what he was there for; and on being told, said, 'They cannot put you there for that.' 'But I am here,' was the laconic answer.

The analogy, then, of man's whole condition in this life might lead us to expect the same system of procedure throughout; that the evidence which substantiates religious truth, and claims religious action, would involve this responsibility as well as that which substantiates other kinds of truth, and demands other kinds of action. And after all, what else, in either case, could answer the purpose, if (as already said) this world be the school of training of man's moral nature? How else could the discipline of his faculties, the exercise of patience, humility, and fortitude, be secured? How, except amidst a state of things less than certainty—whether under the form of that passive faith which mimics the possession of absolute certainty, or absolute certainty itself—could man's nature be trained to combined self-reliance and self-distrust, circumspection and resolution, and, above all, to confidence in God? Man cannot be nursed and dandled into the manhood of his nature, by that unthinking faith which leaves no doubts to be felt, and no objections to be weighed; Nor can his docility ever be tested, if he is never called upon to believe any thing which it would not be an absurdity and contradiction to deny. This species of responsibility, then, not only cannot be dispensed with, but is absolutely necessary; and, consequently, however desirable it may appear that we should have furnished to us that short path to certainty which a pretended infallibility* promises to man, or that equally short path which leads to the same termination, by telling us that we are to believe nothing which we cannot demonstrate to be true, or which, a priori, we may presume to be false, must be a path which leads astray. In the one case, how can the 'reasonable service' which Scripture demands—the enlightened love and conscientious investigation of truth—its reception, not without doubts, but against doubts—how could all this co-exist with a faith which presents the whole sum of religion in the formulary, 'I am to believe without a doubt, and perform without hesitation. whatever my guide, Parson A. tells me?' Not that, even in that case (as has often been shown), the man would be relieved form the necessity of absolutely depending on the dreaded exercise of his private judgment; for he must at least have exercised it once for all (unless each man is to remit his religion wholly to the accident of his birth), and that on two of the most arduous of all questions: first, which of several churches, pretending to infallibility, is truly infallible? And next, whether the man may infallibly regard his worthy Parson A. as an infallible expounder of the infallibility. But, supposing this stupendous difficulty surmounted, though then, it is true, all may seem genuine faith, in reality there is none: where absolute infallibility is supposed to have been attained (even though erroneously), faith, in strict propriety—certainly that faith which is alone of any value as an instrument of man's moral training—which recognises and intelligently struggles with objections and difficulties—is impossible. Men may be said, in such case, to know, but can hardly be said to believe. Before Columbus had seen America, he believed in its existence; but when he had seen it, his faith became knowledge. Equally impossible, and for the same reason, is any place for faith on the opposite hypothesis; for if man is to believe nothing but what his reason can comprehend, and to act only upon evidence which amounts to certainly, the same paradox is true; for when there is no reason to doubt, there can be none to believe. Faith ever stands between conflicting probabilities; but her position is (if we may use the metaphor) the centre of gravity between them, and will be proportionally nearer the greater mass. ____

* See Archbishop Whately's admirable discourse, entitled 'The Search after Infallibility, considered in reference to the Danger of Religious Errors arising within the Church, in the primitive as well as in all later Ages.' He here makes excellent use of the fruitful principle of Butler's great work, by showing that, however desirable, a

priori, an infallible guide would seem to fallible man, God in fact has every where denied it; and that, in denying it in relation to religion, he has acted only as he always acts. ____

In the mean time, that arduous responsibility which attaches to man, and which is obviated neither by an implicit faith in a human infallibility, nor an exclusive reference of that faith to cases in which reason is synonymous with demonstration, that is, to cases which leave no room for it, is at once relieved, and effectually relieved, by the maxim—the key-stone of all ethical truth—that only voluntary error condemns us;—that all we are really responsible for, is a faithful, honest, patient, investigation and weighing of evidence, as far as our abilities and opportunities admit, and a conscientious pursuit of what we honestly deem truth, wherever it may lead us. We concede that a really dispassionate and patient conduct in this respect is what man is too ready to assume he has practised,—and this fallacy cannot be too sedulously guarded against. But that guilty liability to selfdeception, does not militate against the truth of the representation now made. It is his duty to see that he does not abuse the maxim,—that he does not rashly acquiesce in any conclusion that he wishes to be true, or which he is too lazy to examine. If all possible diligence and honesty have been exerted in the search, the statement of Chillingworth, bold as it is, we should not hesitate to adopt, in all the rigour of his own language. It is to the effect, that if 'in him alone there were a confluence of all the errors which have befallen the sincere professors of Christianity, he should not be so much afraid of them, as to ask God's pardon for them;' absolutely involuntary error being justly regarded by him as blameless.

On the other hand, we firmly believe, from the natural relations of truth with the constitution of the mind of man, that, with the exception of a very few cases of obliquity of intellect, which may safely be left to the merciful interpretations and apologies of Him who created such intellects, those who thus honestly and industriously 'seek' shall 'find;'—not all truth, indeed, but enough to secure their safety; and that whatever remaining errors may infest and disfigure the truth they have attained, they shall not be imputed to them for sin. According to the image which apostolic eloquence has employed, the Baser materials which unavoidable haste, prejudice, and ignorance may have incorporated with the gold of the edifice, will be consumed by the fire which 'will try every man's work of what sort it is,' but he himself will be saved amidst those purifying flames. Like the bark which contained the Apostle and the fortunes of the Gospel, the frail vessel may go to pieces on the rocks, 'but by boat or plank' the voyager himself shall 'get safe to shore.'

It is amply sufficient, then, to lighten our responsibility, that we are answerable only for our honest endeavours to discover and to practise the truth; and, in fact, the responsibility is principally felt to be irksome, and man is so prompt by devices of his own, to release himself from it, not on account of any intrinsic difficulty which remains after the above limitations are admitted, but because he wishes to be exempt from that very necessity of patient and honest investigation. It is not so much the difficulty of finding, as the trouble of seeking the truth, from which he shrinks; a necessity, however, from which, as it is an essential instrument of his moral education and discipline, he can never be released.

If the previous representations be true, the conditions of that intelligent faith which God requires from his intelligent offspring, may be fairly inferred to be such as we have already stated;—that the evidence for the truths we are to believe shall be, first, such as our faculties are competent to appreciate, and against which, therefore, the mere negative argument arising from our ignorance of the true solution of such difficulties, as are, perhaps, insoluble because we are finite, can be no reply; and, secondly, such an amount of this evidence as shall fairly overbalance all the objections which we can appreciate. This is the condition to which God has obviously subjected us as inhabitants of this world; and it is on such evidence we are here perpetually acting. We now believe a thousand things we cannot fully comprehend. We may not see the intrinsic evidence of their truth, but their extrinsic evidence is sufficient to induce us unhesitatingly to believe, and to act upon them. When that evidence is sufficient in amount, we allow it to overbear all the individual difficulties and perplexities which hang round the truths to which it is applied, unless, indeed, such difficulties can be proved to involve absolute contradictions; for these, of course, no evidence can substantiate. For example, in a thousand cases, a certain combination of merely circumstantial evidence in favour of a certain judicial decision, is familiarly allowed to vanquish all apparent discrepancy on particular and subordinate points;—the want of concurrence in the evidence of the witnesses on such points shall not cause a shadow of a doubt as to the conclusion. For we feel that it is far more improbable that the conclusion should be untrue, than that the difficulty we cannot solve is truly incapable of a solution; and when the evidence reaches this point the objection no longer troubles us.

It is the same with historic investigations. There are ten thousand facts in history which no one doubts, though the narrators of them may materially vary in their version, and though some of the circumstances alleged may be in appearance inexplicable, but the last thing a man would think of doing, in such cases, would be to neglect the preponderant evidence on account of the residuum of insoluble objections. He does not, in short, allow his ignorance to control his knowledge, nor the evidence which he has not got to destroy what he has; and the less so, that experience has taught him that in many cases such apparent difficulties have been cleared up, in the course of time, and by the progress of knowledge, and proved to be contradictions in appearance only.

It is the same with the conclusions of natural philosophy, when well proved by experiment, however unaccountable for awhile may be the discrepancy with apparently opposing phenomena. No one disbelieves the Copernican theory now; though thousands did for awhile, on what they believed the irrefragable evidence of their senses. Now, let us only suppose the Copernican theory not to have been discovered by human reason, but made known by revelation, and its reception enjoined on faith, leaving the apparent inconsistency with the evidence of the senses just as it was. Thousands, no doubt, would have said, that no such evidence could justify them in disbelieving their own eyes, and that such an insoluble objection was sufficient to overturn the evidence. Yet we now see, in point of fact, that it is not only possible, but true, that the objection was apparent only, and admits of a complete solution. Thousands accordingly receive philosophy—this very philosophy—on testimony which apparently contradicts their senses, without even yet knowing more of it than if it were revealed from heaven. This gives too much reason to suspect, that in other and higher cases, the will has much to do with human scepticism. Nor do we well know what thousands who neglect religion on account of the alleged uncertainty of its evidence could reply, if God were to say to them,

'And yet on such evidence, and that far inferior in degree, you have never hesitated to act, when your own temporal interests were concerned. You never feared to commit the bark of your worldly fortunes to that fluctuating element. In many cases you believed on the testimony of others what seemed even to contradict your own senses. Why were you so much more scrupulous in relation to ME?'

The above examples are fair illustrations, we venture to think, of the conditions under which we are required to believe the far higher truths, attended no doubt with great difficulties, which are authenticated in the pages of the two volumes (Nature and Scripture) which God has put into our hands to study; of the conditions to which He subjects us in training us for a future state, and developing in us the twofold perfection involved in the words 'a reasonable faith.' If the considerations just urged were duly borne in mind, we cannot help thinking that they would afford (where any modesty remained) all answer to most of those forms of unbelief which, from time to time, rise up in the world, and not least in our own day. These are usually founded on one or more supposed insoluble objections, arising out of our ignorance. The probability that they are incapable of solution is rashly assumed, and made to overbear the far stronger probability arising from the positive and appreciable evidence which substantiates the truths involved in those difficulties: a course the more unreasonable inasmuch as—first, many such difficulties might be expected; and, secondly, in analogous cases, we see that many such difficulties have in time disappeared. On the other hand, it is, no doubt much more easy to insist on individual objections, which no man can effectually answer, than it is to appreciate at once the total effect of many lines of argument, and many sources of evidence, all bearing on one point. That difficulty was long ago beautifully stated by Butler*, in a passage well worthy of the reader's perusal; and as Pascal had observed before him, not only is it difficult, but impossible, for the human mind to retain the impression of a large combination of evidence, even if it could for a moment fully realise the collective effect of the whole. But it cannot do even this, any more than the eye can take in at once, in mass and detail, the objects of an extensive landscape. ____

* 'The truth of our religion, like the truth of common matters, is to be judged of by all the evidence taken together. And, unless the whole series of things which may be alleged in this argument, and every particular thing in it, can reasonably be supposing to have been by accident (for here the stress of the argument of Christianity lies), then is the truth of it proved. . . . It is obvious how much advantage the nature of this evidence gives to those persons who attack Christianity, especially in conversation. For it is easy to show in a short and lively manner that such and such things are liable to objection, but impossible to show, in like manner, the united force of the whole argument in one view.'—Analogy, part II. chap. vii.

———

Let us now be permitted briefly to apply the preceding principles to two of the greatest controversies which have exercised the minds of men; that which relates to the existence of God, and that which relates to the truth of Christianity; in both of which, if we mistake not, man's position is precisely similar—placed, that is, amidst evidence abundantly sufficient to justify his reasonable faith, and yet attended with difficulties abundantly sufficient to baffle an indocile reason.

Without entering into the many different sources of argument for the existence of a Supreme Intelligence, we shall only refer to that proof on which all theists, savage and civilised, in some form or other, rely—the traces of an 'eternal power and godhead' in the visible creation. The argument depends on a principle which, whatever may be its metaphysical history or origin, is one which man perpetually recognises, which every act of his own consciousness verifies, which he applies fearlessly to every phenomenon, known or unknown; and it is this,—That every effect has a cause (though he knows nothing of their connexion), and that effects which bear marks of design have a designing cause. This principle is so familiar that if he were to affect to doubt it in any practical case in human life, he would only be laughed at as a fool, or pitied as insane. The evidence, then, which substantiates the greatest and first of truths mainly depends on a principle perfectly familiar and perfectly recognised. Man can estimate the nature of that evidence; and the amount of it, in this instance, he sees to be as vast as the sum of created objects;—nay, far more, for it is as vast as the sum of their relations. So that if (as is apt to be the case) the difficulties of realising this tremendous truth are in proportion to the extent of knowledge and the powers of reflection, the evidence we can perfectly appreciate is cumulative in an equal or still higher proportion. Obvious as are the marks of design in each individual object, the sum of proof is not merely the sum of such indications, but that sum infinitely multiplied by the relations established and preserved amongst all these objects; by the adjustment which harmonises them all into one system, and impresses on all the parts of the universe a palpable order and subordination. While even in a single part of an organised being (as a hand or an eye) the traces of design are not to be mistaken, these are indefinitely multiplied by similar proofs of contrivance in the many individual organs of one such being—as of an entire animal or vegetable. These are yet to be multiplied by the harmonious relations which are established of mutual proportion and subserviency amongst all the organs of any one such being: And as many beings even of that one species or class as there are, so many multiples are there of the same proofs. Similar indications yield similar proofs of design in each individual part, and in the whole individual of all the individuals of every other class of beings; and this sum of proof is again to be multiplied by the proofs of design in the adjustment and mutual dependence and subordination of each of these classes of organised beings to every other, and to all; of the vegetable to the animal—-of the lower animal to the higher. Their magnitudes, numbers, physical force, faculties, functions, duration of life, rates of multiplication and development, sources of subsistence, must all have been determined in exact ratios, and could not transgress certain limits without involving the whole universe in confusion. This amazing sum of probabilities is yet to be further augmented by the fact that all these classes of organised substances are intimately related to those great elements of the material world in which they live, to which they are adapted, and which are adapted to them; that all of them are subject to the influence of certain mighty and subtle agencies which pervade all nature,—and which are of such tremendous potency that any chance error in their proportions of activity would be sufficient to destroy all, and which yet axe exquisitely balanced and inscrutably harmonised.

The proofs of design, arising from the relations thus maintained between all the parts, from the most minute to the most vast, of our own world, are still to be further multiplied by the inconceivably momentous relations subsisting between our own and other planets and their common centre; amidst whose sublime and solemn phenomena science has most clearly discovered that everything is accurately adjusted by geometrical precision of force and movement; where the chances of error are infinite, and the proofs of intelligence, therefore, equal. These proofs of design in each fragment of the universe, and in all combined, are continually further multiplied by every fresh discovery, whether in the minute or the vast—by the microscope or the telescope; for every fresh law that is discovered, being in harmony with all that has previously been discovered, not only yields its own proof of design, but infinitely more, by all the relations in which it stands to other laws: it yields, in fact, as many as there are adjustments which have been effected between itself and all besides. Each new proof of design, therefore, is not a solitary fact; but one which entering as another element into a most complex machinery, indefinitely multiplies the combinations, in any one of which chance might have gone astray. From this infinite array of proofs of design, it seems to man's reason, in ordinary moods, stark madness to account for the phenomena of the universe upon any other supposition than that which docs account, and can alone account, for them all,—the supposition of a Presiding Intelligence, illimitable alike in power and in wisdom.

The only difficulty is justly to appreciate such an argument to obtain a sufficiently vivid impression of such an accumulation of probabilities. This very difficulty, indeed, in some moods, may minister to a temporary doubt. For let us catch man in those moods,—perhaps after long meditation on the metaphysical grounds of human belief,—and he begins to doubt, with unusual modesty, whether the child of dust is warranted to conclude anything on a subject which loses itself in the infinite, and which so far transcends all his powers of apprehension; he begins half to doubt, with Hume, whether he can reason analogically from the petty specimens of human ingenuity to phenomena so vast and so unique; a misgiving which is strengthened by reflecting on all those to him incomprehensible inferences to which the admission of the argument leads

him, and which seem almost to involve contradictions. Let him
ponder for awhile the ideas involved in the notion of Selfsubsist-
ence, Eternity, Creation; Power, Wisdom, and Knowledge, so unlimited as to embrace at once all things, and all their relations, actual
and possible, — this 'unlimited' expanding into a dim apprehension
of the 'infinite'; — of infinitude of attributes, omnipresent in every
point of space, and yet but one and not many infinitudes; — let him
once humbly ponder such incomprehensible difficulties as these,
and he will soon feel that though in the argument from design,
there seemed but one vast scene of triumph for his reason, there is
as large a scene of exertion left for his faith. That faith he ordinarily
yields; he sees it is justified by those proofs of the great truth he can
appreciate, and which he will not allow to be controlled by the difficulties his conscious feebleness cannot solve; and the rather, that he
sees that if he does not accept that evidence, he has equally incomprehensible difficulties to encounter, and two or three stark contradictions into the bargain. His reason, therefore, triumphs in the
proofs, and his faith triumphs over the difficulties.

It is the same with the doctrine of the Divine government of the
world. In ordinary states of mind man counts it an absurdity to
suppose that the Deity would have created a world to abandon it;
that, having employed wisdom and power so vast in its construc-
tion, he would leave it to be the sport of chance. He feels that the
intuitions of right and wrong; the voice of conscience; satisfaction in
well-doing; remorse for crime; the present tendency, at least, of the
laws of the universe, — all point to the same conclusion, while their
imperfect fulfilment equally points to a future and more accurate
adjustment. Yet let the man look exclusively for awhile on the opposite side of the tapestry; let him brood over any of the facts which
seem at war with the above conclusion; on some signal triumph of
baseness and malignity; on oppressed virtue, on triumphant vice;
on 'the wicked spreading himself like a green bay tree;' and especially on the mournfull and inscrutable mystery of the 'Origin of
Evil,' and he feels that 'clouds and darkness' envelope the administration of the Moral Governor, though 'justice and judgment are
the habitation of his throne.' The evidences above mentioned for the
last conclusion are direct and positive, and such as man can appreciate; the difficulties spring from his limited capacity, or imperfect

glimpses of a very small segment of the universal plan. Nor are those difficulties less upon the opposite hypothesis: and they are there further burdened with two or three additional absurdities. The preponderant evidence, far from removing the difficulties, scarcely touches them, — yet it is felt to be sufficient to justify faith, though most abundant faith is required still.

Are the evidences, then, in behalf of Christianity less of a nature which man can appreciate? or can the difficulties involved in its reception be greater than in the preceding cases? If not, and if, moreover, while the evidence turns as before on principles with which we are familiar, the more formidable objections, as before, are such that we are not competent to decide upon their absolute insolubility, we see how man ought to act; that is, not to let his ignorance control his knowledge, but to let his reason accept the proofs which justify his faith, in accepting the difficulties. In no case is he, it appears, warranted to look for the certainty which shall exclude (whatever the triumphs of his reason) a gigantic exercise of his faith. Let us briefly consider a few of the evidences. And in order to give the statement a little novelty, we shall indicate the principal topics of evidence, not by enumerating what the advocate of Christianity believes in believing it to be true, but what the infidel must believe in believing it to be false. The a priori objection to Miracles we shall briefly touch afterwards.

First, then, in relation to the Miracles of the New Testament, whether they be supposed masterly frauds on men's senses committed at the time and by the parties supposed in the records, or fictions (designed or accidental) subsequently fabricated — but still, in either case, undeniably successful and triumphant beyond all else in the history whether of fraud or fiction — the infidel must believe as follows: On the first hypothesis, he must believe that a vast number of apparent miracles — involving the most astounding phenomena — such as the instant restoration of the sick, blind, deaf, and lame, and the resurrection of the dead — performed in open day, amidst multitudes of malignant enemies — imposed alike on all, and triumphed at once over the strongest prejudices and the deepest enmity: — those who received them and those who rejected them differing only in the certainly not very trifling particular — as to whether they came from heaven or from hell. He must believe that those who were thus successful in this extraordinary conspiracy against men's senses and against common sense, were Galilaean Jews, such as all history of the period represents them; ignorant, obscure, illiterate; and, above all, previously bigoted, like all their countrymen, to the very system, of which, together with all other religions on the earth, they modestly meditated the abrogation; he must believe that, appealing to these astounding frauds in the face both of Jews and Gentiles as an open evidence of the truth of a new revelation, and demanding on the strength of them that their countrymen should surrender a religion which they acknowledged to be divine, and that all other nations should abandon their scarcely less venerable systems of superstition, they rapidly succeeded in both these very probable adventures; and in a few years, though without arms, power, wealth, or science, were to an enormous extent victorious over all prejudice, philosophy, and persecution; and in three centuries took nearly undisputed possession, amongst many nations, of the temples of the ejected deities. He must farther believe that the original performers, in these prodigious frauds on the world, acted not only without any assignable motive, but against all assignable motive; that they maintained this uniform constancy in unprofitable falsehoods, not only together, but separately, in different countries, before different tribunals, under all sorts of examinations and cross-examinations, and in defiance of the gyves, the scourge, the axe, the cross, the stake; that these whom they persuaded to join their enterprise, persisted like themselves in the same obstinate belief of the same 'cunningly devised' frauds; and though they had many accomplices in their singular conspiracy, had the equally singular fortune to free themselves and their coadjutors flout all transient weakness towards their cause and treachery towards one another; and, lastly, that these men, having, amidst all their ignorance, originality enough to invent the most pure and sublime system of morality which the world has ever listened to, had, amidst all their conscious villany, the effrontery to preach it, and, which is more extraordinary, the inconsistency to practise it!* _____

* So far as we have any knowledge from history, this must have been the case; and Gibbon fully admits and insists upon it. Indeed, no infidel hypothesis can afford to do without the virtues of the

early Christians in accounting for the success of the falsehoods of Christianity. Hard alternatives of a wayward hypothesis! ____

On the second of the above-mentioned hypothesis, that these miracles were either a congeries of deeply contrived fictions, or accidental myths, subsequently invented, the infidel must believe, on the former supposition, that, though even transient success in literary forgery, when there are any prejudices to resist, is among the rarest of occurrences; yet that these forgeries — the hazardous work of many minds, making the most outrageous pretensions, and necessarily challenging the opposition of Jew and Gentile were successful beyond all imagination, over the hearts of mankind; and have continued to impose, by an exquisite appearance of artless truth, and a most elaborate mosaic of feigned events artfully cemented into the ground of true history, on the acutest minds of different races and different ages; while, on the second supposition, he must believe that accident and chance have given to these legends their exquisite appearance of historic plausibility; and on either supposition, he must believe (what is still more wonderful) that the world, while the fictions were being published, and in the known absence of the facts they asserted to be true, suffered itself to be befooled into the belief of their truth, and out of its belief of all the systems it did previously believe to be true; and that it acted thus notwithstanding persecution from without, as well as prejudice front within; that strange to say the strictest historic investigation bring this compilation of fictions or myths-even by the admission of Strauss himself — within thirty or forty years of the very time in which all the alleged wonders they relate are said to have occurred; wonders which the perverse world knew it had not seen, but which it was determined to believe in spite of evidence, prejudice, and persecution! In addition to all this, the infidel must believe that the men who were engaged in the compilation of these monstrous fictions, chose them as the vehicle of the purest morality; and, though the most pernicious deceivers of mankind were yet the most scrupulous preachers of veracity and benevolence! Surely of him, who can receive all these paradoxes — and they form but a small part of what might be mentioned — we may say, 'O infidel, great is thy Faith!'

On the supposition that neither of these theories, whether of fraud or fiction, will account, if taken by itself, for the whole of the supernatural phenomena, which strew the pages of the New Testament, then the objector, who relies on both, must believe, in turn, both sets of the above paradoxes; and then, with still more reason than before, may we exclaim, 'O infidel, great is thy Faith!'

Again; he must believe that till those apparent coincidences, which seem to connect Prophecy with the facts of the origin and history of Christianity,—some, embracing events too vast for hazardous speculations and others, incidents too minute for it,—are purely fortuitous; that all the cases in which the event seems to tally with the prediction, are mere chance coincidences: and he must believe this, amongst other events, of two of the most unlikely to which human sagacity was likely to pledge itself, and yet which have as undeniably occurred, (and after the predictions) as they were a priori improbable and anomalous in the world's history; the one is that the Jews should exist as a distinct nation in the very bosom of all other nations, without extinction, and without amalgamation,—other nations and even races having so readily melted away under less than half the influence which have been at work upon them*; the other, and opposite paradox,—that a religion, propagated by ignorant, obscure, and penniless vagabonds, should diffuse itself amongst the most diverse nations in spite of all opposition,—it being the rarest of phenomena to find any religion which is capable of transcending the limits of race, clime, and the scene of its historic origin; a religion which, if transplanted, will not die, a religion which is more than a local or national growth of superstition! That such a religion as Christianity should so easily break these barriers, and though supposed to be cradled in ignorance, fanaticism, and fraud, should, without force of arms, and in the face of persecution, 'ride forth conquering and to conquer,' through a long career of victories, defying the power of kings and emptying the temples of deities,—who, but an infidel, has faith enough to believe?+

---

* The case of the Gipsies, often alleged as a parallel, is a ludicrous evasion of the argument. These few and scattered vagabonds, whose very safety has been obscurity and contempt, have never

attracted towards them a thousandth part of the attention, or the hundred thousandth part of the cruelties, which have been directed against the Jews. Had it been otherwise, they would long since have melted away from every country in Europe. We repeat that the existence of a nation for 1800 years in the bosom of all nations, conquered and persecuted, yet never extinguished, and the propagation of a religion amongst different races without force, and even against it, — are both, so far as known, paradoxes in history. + 'They may say,' says Butler, 'that the conformity between the prophecies and the event is by accident; but there are many instances in which such conformity itself cannot be denied.' His whole remarks on the subject, and especially those on the impression to be derived from the multitude of apparent coincidences, in a long series of prophecies, some vast, some minute; and the improbability of their all being accidental are worthy of his comprehensive genius. It is on the effect of the whole, not on single coincidences, that the argument depends. ____

Once more then; if, from the external evidences of this religion, we pass to those which the only records by which we know any thing of its nature and origin supplies, the infidel must believe, amongst other paradoxes, that it is probable that a knot of obscure and despised plebeians — regarded as the scum of a nation which was itself regarded as the scum of all other nations — originated the purest, most elevated, and most influential theory of ethics the world has ever seen; that a system of sublimest truth, expressed with unparalleled simplicity, sprang from ignorance; that precepts enjoining the most refined sanctity were inculcated by imposture; that the first injunctions to universal love broke from the lips of bigotry! He must further believe that these men exemplified the ideal perfection of that beautiful system in the most unique, original, and faultless picture of virtue ever conceived — a picture which has extorted the admiration even of those who could not believe it to be a portrait, and who have yet confessed themselves unable to account for it except as such.* He must believe, too, that these ignorant and fraudulent Galileans voluntarily aggravated the difficulty of their task, by exhibiting their proposed ideal, not by bare enumeration and description of qualities, but by the most arduous of all methods of representation — that of dramatic action; and, what is

more, that they succeeded; that in that representation they under-
took to make him act with sublime consistency in scenes of the most
extraordinary character and the most touching pathos, and utter
moral truth in the most exquisite fictions in which such truth was
ever embodied; and that again they succeeded; that so ineffably rich
in genius were these obscure wretches, that no less than four of
them were found equal to this intellectual achievement; and while
each has told many events, and given many traits which the others
have omitted, that they have all performed their task in the same
unique style of invention and the same unearthly tone of art; that
one and all, while preserving each his own individuality, has, nevertheless, attained a certain majestic simplicity of style unlike any
tiring else (not only in any writings of their own nation, their alleged sacred writings, and infinitely superior to any thing which
their successors, Jews or Christians, though with the advantage of
these models, could ever attain,) but, unlike any acknowledged
human writings in the world, and possessing the singular property
of being capable of ready transfusion, without the loss of a thought
or a grace, into every language spoken by man: he must believe that
these fabricators of fiction, in common with the many other contrib-
utors to the New Testament, most insanely added to the difficulty of
their task by delivering the whole in fragments and in the most
various kinds of composition, — in biography, history, travels, and
familiar letters; incorporating and interfusing with the whole an
amazing number of minute facts, historic allusions, and specific
references to persons, places, and dates, as if for the very purpose of
supplying posterity with the easy means of detecting their imposi-
tions: he must believe that, in spite of their thus encountering what
Paley calls the 'danger of scattering names and circumstances in
writings where nothing but truth can preserve consistency,' they so
happy succeeded, that whole volumes have been employed pointing out their latent and often most recondite congruities; many of
them lying so deep, and coming out after such comparison of various passages and collateral lights, that they could never have an-
swered the purposes of fraud, even if the most prodigious genius
for fraud had been equal to the fabrication; congruities which, in
fact, were never suspected to exist till they were expressly elicited
by the attacks of Infidelity, and were evidently never thought of by
the writers; he must believe that they were profoundly sagacious

enough to construct such a fabric of artful harmonies, and yet such simpletons as, by doing infinitely more than was necessary, to encounter infinite risks of detection, to no purpose; sagacious enough to out-do all that sagacity has ever done, as shown by the effects, and yet not sagacious enough to be merely specious: and finally, he must believe that these illiterate impostors had the art in all their various writings, which evidently proceed from different minds, to preserve the same inimitable marks of reality, truth, and nature in their narrations—the miraculous and the ordinary alike—and to assume and preserve, with infinite case, amidst their infinite impostures, the tone and air of undissembled earnestness.+ ____

* To Christ alone, of all the characters ever portrayed to man, belongs that assemblage of qualities which equally attract love and veneration; to him alone belong in perfection those rare traits which the Roman historian, with affectionate flattery, attributes too absolutely to the merely mortal object of his eulogy: 'Nec illi, quod est rarissimum aut facilitas auctoritatem, aut severitas amorem, deminuit.' Still more beautiful is the Apostles description of superiority to all Human failings, with ineffable pity for human sorrows: 'He can be touched with the feelings of our infirmities, though without sin.' + Was there ever in truth a man who could read the appeals of Paul to his converts, and doubt either that the letters were real or that the man was in earnest? We scarcely venture to think it. ____

If, on the other hand, he supposes that all the congruities of which we have spoken, were the effect not of fraudulent design, but of happy accident,—that they arranged themselves in spontaneous harmony—he must believe that chance has done what even the most prodigious powers of invention could not do. And lastly, he must believe that these same illiterate men, who were capable of so much, were also capable of projecting a system of doctrine singularly remote from all ordinary and previous speculation; of discerning the necessity of taking under their special patronage those passive virtues which man least loved, and found it must difficult to cultivate; and of exhibiting, in their preference of the spiritual to the ceremonial, and their treatment of many of the most delicate questions of practical ethics and casuistry, a justness and elevation of sentiment as alien as possible from the superstition and fanaticism

of their predecessors who had corrupted the Law—and the superstition and fanaticism of their followers very soon corrupted the
Gospel; and that they, and they alone, rose above the strong tendencies to the extravagances which had been so conspicuous during the
past, and were soon to be as conspicuous in the future.—These and
a thousand other paradoxes (arising out of the supposition that
Christianity is the fraudulent or fictitious product of such an age,
country, and, above all, such men as the problem limits us to), must
the infidel receive, and receive all at once; and of him who can receive them we can but once more declare that so far 'from having no
faith', he rather possesses the 'faith' which removes 'mountains!'—
only it appears that his faith, like that of Rome or of Oxford, is a
faith which excludes reason.

On the other hand, to him who accepts Christianity, none of these
paradoxes present themselves. On the supposition of the truth of
the miracles and the prophecies, he does not wonder at its origin or
success: and as little does he wonder at all the literary and intellectual achievements of its early chroniclers—if their elevation of sentiment was from a divine source, and if the artless harmony, and
reality of their narratives was the simple effect of the consistency of
truth, and of transcription from the life.

Now, on the other hand, what are the chief objections which Rec-
oncile the infidel to his enormous burden of paradoxes, and which
appear to the Christian far less invincible than the paradoxes themselves? They are, especially with all modern infidelity, objections to
the a priori improbability of the doctrines revealed, and of the miracles which sustain them. Now, here we come to the very distinction
on which we have already insisted, and which is so much insisted
on by Butler. The evidence which sustains Christianity is all such as
man is competent to consider; and is precisely of the same nature as
that which enters into his every-day calculations of probability;
While the objections are founded entirely on our ignorance and
presumption. They suppose that we know more of the modes of the
divine administration—of what God may have permitted, of what is
possible and impossible to the ultimate development of an imper-
fectly developed system, and its relations to the entire universe,—
than we do or can know.* ___

* The possible implications of Christianity with distant regions of the universe, and the dim hints which hints which Scripture seems to throw out as to such implication, are beautifully treated in the 4th, 5th, and 6th of Chalmer's 'Astronomical Discourses;' and we need not tell the read of Butler how much he insists upon similar considerations. ____

Of these objections the most widely felt and the most specious, especially in our day, is the assumption that miracles are an impossibility+; and yet we will venture to say that there is none more truly unphilosophical. That miracles are improbable viewed in relation to the experience of the individual or of the mass of men, is granted; for if they were not, they would, as Paley says, be no miracles; an every-day miracle is none. But that they are either impossible or so improbable that, if they were wrought, no evidence could establish them, is another matter. The first allegation involves a curious limitation of omnipotence; and the second affirms in effect, that, if God were to work a miracle, it would be our duty to disbelieve him! ___

+ It is, as we shall see, the avowed axiom of Strauss; he even acknowledges, that if it be not true, he would not think it worth while to discredit the history of the Evangelists; that is, the history must be discredited, because he has resolved that a miracle is an impossibility! ____

We repeat our firm conviction that this a priori assumption against miracles is but a vulgar illusion of one of Bacon's idola tribus. So far from being disposed to admit the principle that a 'miracle is an impossibility,' we shall venture on what may seem to some a paradox, but which we are convinced is a truth,—that time will come, and is coming, when even those who shall object to the evidence which sustains the Christian miracles will acknowledge that philosophy requires them to admit that men have no ground whatever to dogmatise on the antecedent impossibility of miracles in general; and that not merely because if theists at all, they will see the absurdity of the assertion, while they admit that the present order of things had a beginning; and, if Christians at all, the equal absurdity of the assertion, while they admit that it will have an end;—not only because the geologist will have familiarised the world with the idea of successive interventions, and, in fact, distinct creative acts, having all the nature of miracles;—not only, we say, for these special reasons, but for a more general one. The true philosopher will see that, with his limited experience and that of all his contemporaries, he has no right to dogmatise about all that may have been permitted or will be permitted in the Divine administration of the universe; he will see that those who with one voice denied, about half a century ago, the existence of aerolites, and summarily dismissed all the alleged facts as a silly fable, because it contradicted their experience,—that those who refused to admit the Copernican theory because, as they said, it manifestly contradicted their experience,—that the schoolboy who refuses to admit the first law of motion because, as he says, it gives the lie to all his experience,—that the Oriental prince (whose scepticism Hume vainly attempts, on his principle, to meet) who denied the possibility of ice because it contradicted his experience,—and, in the same manner, that the men who, with Dr. Strauss, lay down the dictum that a miracle is impossible and a contradiction because it contradicts their experience,—have all been alike contravening the first principles of the modest philosophy of Bacon, and have fallen into one of the most ordinary illusions against which he has warned us namely, that that cannot be true which seems in contradiction to our own experience. We confidently predict that the day will come when the favourite argument of many so called philosopher in this matter will be felt to be the philosophy of the vulgar only; and that though many may, even then, deny that the testimony which supports the Scripture miracles is equal to the task, they will all alike abandon the axiom which supersedes the necessity of at all examining such evidence, by asserting that no evidence can establish them.

While on this subject, we may notice a certain fantastical tone of depreciation of miracles as an evidence of Christianity, which is occasionally adopted even by some who do not deny the possibility or probability, or even the fact, of their occurrence. They affirm them to be of little moment, and represent them—with an exquisite affectation of metaphysical propriety—as totally incapable of convincing men of any moral truth; upon the ground that there is no natural relation between any displays of physical power and any such truth. Now without denying that the nature of the doctrine is a criterion, and must be taken into account in judging of the reality of any alleged miracle, we have but two things to reply to this: first, that, as Paley says in relation to the question whether any accumulation of testimony can establish a miraculous fact, we are content 'to try the theorem upon a simple case,' and affirm that man is so constituted that if he himself sees the blind restored to sight and the dead raised, under such circumstances as exclude all doubt of fraud on the part of others and all mistake on his own, he will uniformly associate authority with such displays of superhuman power; and, secondly, that the notion in question is in direct contravention of the language and spirit of Christ himself, who expressly suspends his claims to men's belief and the authority of his doctrine on the fact of his miracles. 'The works that I do in my Father's name, they bear witness of me.' 'If ye believe not me, believe my works.' 'If I had not come among them, and done the works that none other man did, they had not had sin; but now they have no cloak for their sin.'

We have enumerated some of the paradoxes which infidelity is required to believe; and the old-fashioned, open, intelligible infidelity of the last century accepted them, and rejected Christianity accordingly. That was a self-consistent, simple, Ingenuous thing, compared with those monstrous forms of credulous reason, incredulous faith, metaphysical mysticism, even Christian Pantheism — so many varieties of which have sprung out of the incubation of German rationalism and German philosophy upon the New Testament. The advocates of these systems, after adopting the most formidable of the above paradoxes of infidelity, and (notwithstanding the frequent boast of originality) depending mainly on the same objections, and defending them by the very same critical arguments*, delude themselves with the idea that they have but purified and embalmed Christianity; not aware that they have first made a mummy of it. They are so greedy of paradox, that they, in fact, aspire to be Christians and infidels at the same time. Proclaiming the miracles of Christianity to be illusions of imagination or mythical legends, — the inspiration of its records no other or greater than that of Homer's 'Iliad,' or even 'Aesop's Fables;' — rejecting the whole of that supernatural clement with which the only records which can tell us any thing about the matter are full; declaring its whole history so uncertain that the ratio of truth to error must be a vanishing

fraction;—the advocates of these systems yet proceed to rant and
rave—they are really the only words we know which can express
our sense of their absurdity—in a most edifying vein about the di-
vinity of Christianity, and to reveal to us its true glories. 'Christ,'
says Strauss, 'is not an individual, but an idea; that is to say, humanity. In the human race behold the God-made-man! behold the child
of the visible virgin and the invisible Father!—that is, of matter and
of mind; behold the Saviour, the Redeemer, the Sinless One; behold
him who dies, who is raised again, who mounts into the heavens I
Believe in this Christ! In his death, his resurrection, man is justified
before God!'+

________

* The main objection, both with the old and the new forms of infidelity, is, that against the miracles; the main argument with both,
those which attempt to show their antecedent impossibility; and
criticism directed against the credulity of the records which contain
them. The principal difference is, that modern infidelity shrinks
from the coarse imputation of fraud and imposture on the founders
of Christianity; and prefers the theory of illusion or myth to that of
deliberate fraud. But with this exception, which touches only the
personal character of the founders of Christianity, the case remains
the same. The same postulates and the same arguments are made to
yield substantially the same conclusion. For, all that is supernatural
in Christianity and all credibility in its records, vanish equally on
either assumption. Nor is even the modern mode of interpreting
many of the miracles (as illusions or legends) unknown to the older
infidelity; only it more consistently felt that neither the one theory
nor the other, could be trusted to alone. Velis et remis was its motto.
+ Such is Quinet's brief statement of Strauss's mystico-mythical
Christiantity, founded on the Hegelian philosophy. For a fuller, we
dare not say a more intelligible, account of it in Strauss's own
words, and the metaphysical mysteries on which it depends, the
reader may consult Dr. Beard's translation;—pp. 44, 45. of his Essay
entitled 'Strauss, Hegel, and their Opinions. _____

Whether it be the Rationalism of Paulus, or the Rationalism of
Strauss—whether that which declares all that is supernatural in
Christianity (forming the bulk of its history) to be illusion, or that

which declares it myth, — the conclusions can be made out only by a system of interpretation which can be compared to nothing but the wildest dreams and allegorical systems of some of the early Fathers#; while the results themselves are either those elementary principles of ethics for which there was no need to invoke a revelation at all, or some mystico-metaphysical philosophy, expressed in language as unintelligible as the veriest gibberish of the Alexandrian Platonists. In fact, by such exegesis and by such philosophy, any thing may be made out of any thing; and the most fantastical data be compelled to yield equally fantastical conclusions. ____

# Of the mode of accounting for the supernatural occurrences in the Scriptures by the illusion produced by mistaken natural phenomena, (perhaps the most stupidly jejune of all the theories ever projected by man), Quinet eloquently says, 'The pen which wrote the Provincial Letters would be necessary to lay bare the strange consequences of this theology. According to its conclusion, the tree of good and evil was nothing but a venomous plant, probably a manchineal tree, under which our first parents fell asleep. The shining face of Moses on the heights of Mount Sinai was the natural result of electricity; the vision of Zachariah was effected by the smoke of the chandeliers in the temple; the Magian kings, with their offerings of myrrh, of gold, and of incense, were three wandering merchants, who brought some glittering tinsel to the Child of Bethlehem; the star which went before them a servant bearing a flambeau; the angels in the scene of the temptation, a caravan traversing the desert, laden with provisions; the two angels in the tomb, clothed in white linen, an illusion caused by a linen garment; the Transfiguration, a storm.' Who would not sooner be an old-fashioned infidel than such a doting and maundering rationalist?

——

But the first and most natural question to ask is obviously this: how any mortal can pretend to extract any thing certain, much more divine, from records, the great bulk of which he has reduced to pure frauds, illusions, or legends, — and the great bulk of the remainder to an absolute uncertainty of how little is true and how much false?* Surely it would need nothing less than a new revelation to reveal this sweeping restriction of the old; and we should then be left in an ecstasy of astonishment-first, that the whole significance of it should have been veiled in frauds, illusions, or fictions; secondly, that its true meaning should have been hidden from the world for eighteen hundred years after its divine promulgation; thirdly, that it should be revealed at last, either in results which needed no revelation to reveal them, or in the Egyptian darkness of the allegorieo-metaphysico-mystico-logico-transendental, 'formulae' of the most obscure and contentious philosophy ever devised by man; and lastly, that all this superfluous trouble is to give us, after all, only the mysteries of a most enigmatical philosophy: For of Hegel, in particular, we think it may with truth be said that the reader is seldom fortunate enough to know that he knows his meaning, or even to know that Hegel knew his own. ____

* Daub naively enough declares that, if you except all that relates to angels, demons, and miracle, there is scarcely any mythology in the Gospel.' An exception which reminds one of the Irish prelate who, on reading 'Gulliver's Travels,' remarked that there were some things in that book which he could not think true. ____

Whether, then, we regard the original compilers of the evangelic records as inventing all that Paulus or Strauss rejects, or sincerely believing their own delusions, or that their statements have been artfully corrupted or unconsciously disguised, till Christ and his Apostles are as effectually transformed and travestied as these dreamers are pleased to imagine, with what consistency can we believe any thing certain amidst so many acknowledged fictions inseparably incorporated with them? If A has told B truth once and falsehood fifty times, (wittingly or unwittingly,) what can induce B to believe that he has any reason to believe A in that only time in which he does believe him, unless he knows the same truth by evidence quite independent of A, and for which he is not indebted to him at all? Should we not, then, at once acknowledge the futility of attempting to educe any certain historic fact, however meagre, or any doctrine, whether intelligible or obscure, from documents nine tenths of which are to be rejected as a tissue of absurd fictions? Or why should we not fairly confess that, for aught we can tell, the whole is a fiction? For certainly, as to the amount of historic fact which these men affect to leave, it is obviously a matter of the most trivial importance whether we regard the whole Bible as absolute fiction or not. Whether an obscure Galilean teacher, who taught a moral system which may have been as good (we can never know from such corrupt documents that it was as good) as that of Confucius, or Zoroaster, ever lived or not; and whether we are to add another name to those who have enunciated the elementary truths of ethics, is really of very little moment. Upon their principles we can clearly know nothing about him except that he is the centre of a vast mass of fictions, the invisible nucleus of a huge conglomerate of myths. A thousand times more, therefore, do we respect those, as both more honest and more logical, who, on similar grounds, openly reject Christianity altogether; and regard the New Testament, and speak of it, exactly as they would of Homer's 'Iliad,' or Virgil's 'Aeneid.' Such men, consistently enough, trouble themselves not at all in ascertaining what residuum of truth, historical or critical, may remain in a book which certainly gives ten falsehoods for one truth, and welds both together in inextricable confusion. The German infidels, on the other hand, with infinite labour, and amidst infinite uncertainties, extract either truth 'as old as the creation,' and as universal as human reason,—or truth which, after being hidden from the world for eighteen hundred years in mythical obscurity, is unhappily lost again the moment it is discovered, in the infinitely deeper darkness of the philosophy of Hegel and Strauss; who in vain endeavour to gasp out, in articulate language, the still latent mystery of the Gospel! Hegel, in his last hours, is said to have said,—and if he did not say, he ought to have said,—'Alas! there is but one man in all Germany who understands my doctrine,—and he does not understand it!' And yet, by his account, Hegelianism and Christianity, 'in their highest results,' [language, as usual, felicitously obscure] 'are one.' Both, therefore, are, alas! now for ever lost.

That great problem—to account for the origin and establishment Of Christianity in the world, with a denial at the same time of its miraculous pretensions—a problem, the fair solution of which is obviously incumbent on infidelity—has necessitated the most gratuitous and even contradictory hypotheses, and may safely be said still to present as hard a knot as ever. The favourite hypothesis, recently, has been that of Strauss—frequently re-modified and re-adjusted indeed by himself—that Christianity is a myth, or collection of myths—that is, a conglomerate (as geologists would say) of a very slender portion of facts and truth, with an enormous accretion of undesigned fiction, fable, and superstitions; gradually framed and insensibly received, like the mythologies of Greece and Rome, or the ancient systems of Hindoo theology. It is true, indeed, that the particular critical arguments, the alleged historic discrepancies and so forth, on which this author founds his conclusion—are for the most part, not original; most of them having been insisted on before, both in Germany, and especially in our own country during the Deistical controversies of the preceding century. His idea of myths, however, may be supposed original; and he is very welcome to it. For of all the attempted solutions of the great problem, this will be hereafter regarded as, perhaps, the most untenable. Gibbon, in solving the same problem, and starting in fact from the same axioms,—for he too endeavoured to account for the intractable phenomenon—on natural causes alone,—assigned, as one cause, the reputation of working miracles, the reality of which he denied; but he was far too cautious to decide whether the original thunders of Christianity had pretended to work miracles, and had been enabled to cheat the world into the belief of them, or whether the world had been pleased universally to cheat itself into that belief. He was far too wise to tie himself to the proof that in the most enlightened period of the world's history—amidst the strongest contrarieties of national and religious feeling—amidst the bitterest bigotry of millions in behalf of what was old, and the bitterest contempt of millions of all that was new—amidst the opposing forces of ignorance and prejudice on the one hand and philosophy and scepticism on the other—amidst all the persecutions which attested and proved those hostile feelings on the part of the bulk of mankind—and above all, in the short space of thirty years (which is all that Dr. Stauss allows himself),—Christianity could be thus deposited, like the mythology of Greece and Rome! These, he knew, were very gradual and silent formations; originating in the midst of a remote antiquity and an unhistoric age, during the very infancy and barbarism of the races which adopted them, confined, be it remembered, to those races alone; and displaying, instead of the exquisite and symmetrical beauty of Christianity, those manifest signs of gradual accretion which were fairly to be expected; in the varieties of the deposited or irrupted substances—in the diffracted appearance of various parts—in the very weather stains, so to speak, which mark the whole mass.

That the prodigious aggregate of miracles which the New Testament asserts, would, if fabulous, pass unchallenged, elude all detection, and baffle all scepticism. — collect in the course of a few years energetic and zealous assertors of their reality, in the heart of every civilised and almost every barbarous community, and in the course of three centuries, change the face of the world and destroy every other myth which fairly came in contact with it, — who but Dr. Strauss can believe? Was there no Dr. Strauss in those days? None to question and detect, as the process went on, the utter baselessness of these legends? Was all the world doting — was even the persecuting world asleep? Were all mankind resolved on befooling themselves? Are men wont thus quietly to admit miraculous pretensions, whether they be prejudiced votaries of another system or sceptics as to all? No: whether we consider the age, the country, the men assigned for the origin of these myths, we see the futility of the theory. It does not account even for their invention, much less for their success. We see that if any mythology could in such an age have germinated at all, it must have been one very different from Christianity; whether we consider the sort of Messiah the Jews expected, or the hatred of all Jewish Messiahs, which the Gentiles could not but have felt. The Christ offered them so far from being welcome, was to the one a 'stumbling block' and to the other 'foolishness'; and yet he conquered the prejudices of both.

Let us suppose a parallel myth — if we may abuse the name. Let us suppose the son of some Canadian carpenter aspiring to be a moral teacher, but neither working nor pretending to work miracles; as much hated by his countrymen as Jesus Christ was hated by his, and both he and his countrymen as much hated by all the civilised world beside, as were Jesus Christ and the Jews: let us further suppose him forbidding his followers the use of all force in propagating his doctrine's, and then let us calculate the probability of an unnoticed and accidental deposit, in thirty short years, of a prodigious accumulation about these simple facts. of supernatural but universally accredited fables, these legends escaping detection or suspicion as they accumulated, and suddenly laying hold in a few years of myriads of votaries in all parts of both worlds, and in three centuries uprooting and destroying Christianity and all opposing systems! How long will it be before the Swedenborgian, or the

Mormonite, or any such pretenders, will have similar success? Have there not been a thousand such, and has any one of them had the slightest chance against systems in possession, — against the strongly rooted prejudices of ignorance and the Argus-eyed investigations of scepticism? But all these were opposed to the pretensions of Christianity; nor can any one example of at all similar sudden success be alleged, except in the case of Mahomet; and to that the answer is brief. The history of Mahomet is the history of a conqueror — and his logic was the logic of the sword.

In spite of the theory of Strauss, therefore, not less than that of Gibbon, the old and ever recurring difficulty of giving a rational account of the origin and establishment of Christianity still presents itself for solution to the infidel, as it always has done, and, we venture to say, always will do. It is an insoluble phenomenon, except by the admission of the facts of the — New Testament. 'The miracles,' says Butler, 'are a satisfactory account of the events, of which no other satisfactory account can be given; nor any account at all, but what is imaginary merely and invented.'

In the meantime, the different theories of unbelief mutually refute one another; and we may plead the authority of one against the authority of another. Those who believe Strauss believe both the theory of imposture and the theory of illusion improbable; and those who believe in the theory of imposture believe the theory of myths improbable. And both parties, we are glad to think, are quite right in the judgment they form of one another.

But what must strike every one who reflects as the most surprising thing in Dr. Strauss, is, that with the postulatum with which he sets out, and which he modestly takes for granted as too evident to need proof, he should have thought it worth while to write two bulky volumes of minute criticism on the subject. A miracle he declares to be an absurdity, an contradiction, an impossibility. If we believed this, we should deem a very concise enthymene (after having proved that postulatum though) all that it was necessary to construct on the subject. A miracle cannot be true; ergo, Christianity, which in the only records by which we know anything about it, avows its absolute dependence upon miracles, must be false.

It is a modification of one or other of these monstrous forms of unbelieving belief and Christian infidelity, that Mr. Foxton, late of Oxford, has adopted in his 'Popular Christianity;' as perhaps also Mr. Froude in his 'Nemesis.' It is not very easy, indeed, to say what Mr. Foxton positively believes; having, like his German prototypes, a greater facility of telling what he does believe, and of wrapping up what he does believe in a most impregnable mysticism. He certainly rejects, however, all that which, when rejected a century ago, left, in the estimate of every one, an infidel in puris naturalibus. Like his German acquaintances, he accepts the infidel paradoxes—only, like them, he will still be a Christian. He believes, with Strauss, that a miracle is an impossibility and contradiction—'incredible per se.' As to the inspiration of Christ—he regards it as, in its nature, the same as that of Zoraster, Confucius, Mahomet, Plato, Luther, and Wickliffe—a curious assortment of 'heroic souls.'(Pp. 62, 63.) With a happy art of confusing the 'gifts of genius' no matter whether displayed in intellectual or moral power, and of forgetting that other men are not likely to overlook the difference, he complacently declares 'the wisdom of Solomon and the poetry of Isaiah the fruit of the same inspiration which is popularly attributed to Milton or Shakspeare, or even to the homely wisdom of Benjamin Franklin' (P. 72.) in the same pleasant confusion of mind, he thinks that the 'pens of Plato, of Paul and of Dante, the pencils of Raphael and of Claude, the Chisels of Canova and of Chantrey, no less than the voices of Knox of Wickliffe, and of Luther are ministering instruments, in different degrees, of the same spirit.' (P. 77.) He thinks that 'we find, both in the writers and the records of Scripture, every evidence of human infirmity that can possibly be conceived; and yet we are to believe that God himself specially inspired them with false philosophy, vicious logic, and bad grammar.'(P. 74.) He denies the originality both of the Christian ethic (which he says are a gross plagiarism from Plato) as also in great part of the system of Christian doctrine.* Nevertheless, it would be quite a mistake, it seems, to suppose that Mr. Foxton is no Christian! He is, on the contrary, of the very few who can tell us what Christianity really is; and who can separate the falsehoods and the myths which have so long disguised it. He even talks most spiritually and with an edifying onction. He tells us "God was," indeed, "in Christ, reconciling the world unto himself." And but little deduction need be made from the rapturous language of

Paul, who tells us that "in him dwelt all the fullness of the Godhead bodily" (P. 65); I concede to Christ' (generous admission!) 'the highest inspiration hitherto granted to the prophets of God' (P. 143),—Mahomet, it appears, and Zoroaster and Confucius, having also statues in his truly Catholic Pantheon. 'The position of Christ,' he tells us in another place, is 'simply that of the foremost man in all the world,' though he 'soars far above "all principalities and powers"—above all philosophies hitherto known—above all creeds hitherto propagated in his name'—the true Christian doctrine, after having been hid from ages and generations, being reserved to be disclosed, we presume, by Mr. Foxton. His spiritualism, as usual with the whole school of our new Christian infidels, is, of course, exquisitely refined,—but, unhappily, very vague. He is full of talk of 'a deeep insight,'—of a 'faith not in dead histories, but living realities—a revelation to our innermost nature.' 'The true seer,' he says, 'looking deep into causes, carries in his heart the simple wisdom of God. The secret harmonies of Nature vibrate on his ear, and her fair proportions reveal themselves to his eye. He has a deep faith in the truth of God.' (P. 146.) 'The inspired man is one whose outward life derives all its radiance from the light within him. He walks through stony places by the light of his own soul, and stumbles not. No human motive is present to such a mind in its highest exultation—no love of praise—no desire of fame—no affection, no passion mingles with the divine afflatus, which passes over without ruffling the soul.' (P. 44.) And a great many fine phrases of the same kind, equally innocent of all meaning. ____

   * (Pp. 51—60.) We are hardly likely to yield to Mr. Foxton in our love of Plato, for whom we have expressed, and that very recently, (April, 1848,) no stinted admiration: and what we have there affirmed we are by no means disposed to retract,—that no ancient author has approached, in the expression of ethical truth, so near to the maxims and sometimes the very expressions, of the Gospel. Nevertheless, we as strongly affirm, that he who contrasts (whatever the occasional sublimity of expression) the faltering and often sceptical tone of Plato on religious subjects, with the uniformity and decision of the Evangelical system,—his dark notions in relation to God (candidly confessed) with the glorious recognition of Him in the Gospel as 'our Father,'—his utterly absurd application of his

general principles of morals, in his most Utopian of all Republics, with the broad, plain social ethics of Christianity,—the tone of mournful familiarity (whatever his personal immunity) in which he too often speaks of the saddest pollutions that ever degraded humanity, with the spotless purity of the Christian rule of life,—the hesitating, speculative tone of the Master of the Academy with the decision and majesty of Him who 'spake with authority, and not as the Scribes,' whether Greek or Jewish.—the metaphysical and abstract character of Plato's reasonings with the severely practical character of Christ's,—the feebleness of the motives supplied by the abstractions of the one, and the intensity of those supplied by the other,—the adaptation of the one to the intelligent only, and the adaptation of the other to universal humanity,—the very manner of Plato, his gorgeous style, with the still more impressive simplicity of the Great Teacher,—must surely see in the contrast every indication, to say nothing of the utter gratuitousness (historically) of the contrary hypothesis, that the sublime ethics of the Gospel, whether we regard substance, or manner, or, tone, or style, are no plagiarism from Plato. As for the man who can hold such a notion, he must certainly be very ignorant either of Plate or of Christ. As the best apology for Mr. Foxton's offensive folly we may, perhaps, charitably hope that he is nearly ignorant of both.—Equally absurd is the attempt to identify the metaphysical dreams of Plato with the doctrinal system of the Gospel, though it is quite true, that long subsequent to Christ the Platonising Christians tried to accommodate the speculations of the sage they loved, to the doctrines of a still greater master. But Plato never extorted from his friends stronger eulogies than Christ has often extorted from his enemies.

———

It is amazing and amusing to see with what case Mr. Foxton decides points which have filled folios of controversy. 'In the teaching of Christ himself, there is not the slightest allusion to the modern evangelical notion of an atonement.' 'The diversities of "gifts" to which Paul alludes, Cor. i. 12. are nothing more than those different "gifts" which, in common parlance, we attribute to the various tempers and talents of men.' (P. 67.) 'It is, however, after all, absurd to suppose that the miracles of the Scriptures are subjects of actual belief; either to the vulgar or the learned.' (P. 104.) What an easy time of it must such an all-sufficient controvertist have!

He thinks it possible; too, that Christ, though nothing more than an ordinary man, may really have 'thought himself Divine,' without being liable to the charge of a visionary self-idolatry or of blasphemy,—as supposed by every body, Trinitarian or Unitarian, except Mr. Foxton. He accounts for it by the 'wild sublimity of human emotion, when the rapt spirit first feels the throbbings of the divine afflatus,' &c. &c. A singular afflatus which teaches a man to usurp the name and prerogatives of Deity, and a strange 'inspiration' which inspires him with so profound an ignorance of his own nature! This interpretation, we believe, is peculiarly Mr. Foxton's owe.

The way in which he disposes of the miracles, is essentially that of a vulgar, undiscriminating, unphilosophic mind. There have been, he tells us in effect, so many false miracles, superstitious stories of witches, conjurors, ghosts, hobgoblins, of cures by royal touch, and the like,—and therefore the Scripture miracles are false! Why, who denies that there have been plenty of false miracles? And there have been as many false religions. Is there, therefore, none true? The proper business in every such case is to examine fairly the evidence, and not to generalise after this absurd fashion. Otherwise we shall never believe any thing; for there is hardly one truth that has not its half score of audacious counterfeits.

Still he is amusingly perplexed, like all the rest of the infidel world, how to get rid of the miracles—whether on the principle of fraud, or fiction, or illusion. He thinks there would be 'a great accession to the ranks of reason and common sense by disproving the reality of the miracles, without damaging the veracity or honestly of the simple, earnest, and enthusiastic writers by whom they are recorded;' and complains of the coarse and undiscriminating criticism of most of the French and English Deists, who explain the miracles 'on the supposition of the grossest fraud acting on the grossest credulity.' But he soon finds that the materials for such a compromise are utterly intractable. He thinks that the German Rationalists have depended too much on some 'single hypothesis, which often proves to be insufficient to meet the great variety of conditions and circumstances with which the miracles have been handed down to us.'

Very true; but what remedy? 'We find one German writer endeavouring to explain away the miracles on the mystical (mythical) theory; and another riding into the arena of controversy on the miserable hobby-horse of "clairvoyance" or "mesmerism"; each of these, and a host of others of the same class, rejecting whatever light is thrown on the question by all the theories together.' He therefore proposes, with great and gratuitous liberality, to heap all these theories together, and to take them as they are wanted; not withholding any of the wonders of modern science—even, as would seem, the possible knowledge of 'chloroform' (PP. 104.. 86, 87.)—from the propagators of Christianity!

But, alas! the phenomena are still intractable. The stubborn 'Book' will still baffle all such efforts to explain it away; it is willing to be rejected, if it so pleases men, but it guards itself from being thus made a fool of. For who can fail to see that neither all or any considerable part of the multifarious miracles of the New Testament can be explained by any such gratuitous extension of ingenious fancies; and that if they could be so explained, it would be still impossible to exculpate the men who need such explanations from the charge of perpetuating the grossest frauds! Yet this logical ostrich, who am digest all these stones, presumptuously declares a miracle an impossibility and the very notion of it a contradiction.* But enough of Mr. Foxton.

———

* Mr. Foxton denies that men, in Paley's 'single case in which he tries the general theorem,' would believe the miracle; but he finds it convenient to leave out the most significant circumstances on which Paley makes the validity of the testimony to depend, instead of stating them fairly in Paley's own words. Yet that the sceptics (if such there could be) must be the merest fraction of the species, Mr. Foxton himself immediately proceeds to prove by showing what is undeniably the case) that almost all mankind readily receive miraculous occurrences on far lower evidence than Paley's common sense would require them to demand. Surely he must be related to the Irishman who placed his ladder against the bough he was cutting off. I

———

There are no doubt some minds amongst us, whose power we admit, and whose perversion of power we lament, who have bewildered themselves by really deep meditation on inexplicable mysteries; who demand certainty where certainty is not given to man, or demand for truths which are established by sufficient evidence, other evidence than those truths will admit. We can even painfully sympathise in that ordeal of doubt which such powerful minds are peculiarly exposed—with their Titanic struggles against the still mightier power of Him who has said to the turbulent intellect of man, as well as to the stormy ocean 'Hitherto shalt thou come, but no farther,—and here shall thy proud waves be staid.' We cannot wish better to any such agitated mind than that it may listen to those potent and majestic words: 'Peace—be still!' uttered by the voice of Him who so suddenly hushed the billows of the Galilean lake.

But we are at the same time fully convinced that in our day there are thousands of youths who are falling into the same errors and perils from sheer vanity and affectation; who admire most what they least understand, and adopt all the obscurities and paradoxes they stumble upon, as a cheap path to a reputation for profundity; who awkwardly imitate the manner and retail the phrases of the writers they study; and, as usual, exaggerate to caricature their least agreeable eccentricities. We should think that some of these more powerful minds must be by this time ashamed of that ragged regiment of shallow thinkers, and obscure writers and talkers who at present infest our literature, and whose parrot-like repetition of their own stereotyped phraseology, mingled with some barbarous infusion of half Anglicised German, threatens to form as odious a cant as ever polluted the stream of thought or disfigured the purity of language. Happily it is not likely to be more than a passing fashion; but still it is a very unpleasant fashion while it lasts. As in Johnson's day, every young writer imitated as well as he could the ponderous diction and everlasting antitheses of the great dictator as in Byron's day, there were thousands to whom the world 'was a blank' at twenty or thereabouts, and of whose dark imaginings,' as Macaulay says, the waste was prodigious; so now there are hundreds of dilettanti pantheists', mystics and sceptics to whom everything is a 'sham,' an 'unreality'; Who tell us that the world stands in need of a great 'prophet,' a seer,' a 'true prophet', a large soul,' a god-like soul,'*—who shall dive into 'the depths of the human conscious-ness,' and whose 'utterances' shall rouse the human mind from the 'cheats and frauds' which have hitherto everywhere practised on its simplicity. The tell us, in relation to philosophy, religion, and espe-cially in relation to Christianity, that all that has been believed by mankind has been believed only on 'empirical' grounds; and that the old answers to difficulties will do no longer. They shake their sage heads at such men as Clarke, Paley, Butler, and declare that such arguments as theirs will not satisfy them.,—We are glad to admit that all this vague pretension is now but rarely displayed with the scurrilous spirit of that elder unbelief against which the long series of British apologists for Christianity arose between 1700 and 1750; But there is often in it an arrogance as real, though not in so offensive a form. Sometimes the spirit of unbelief even assumes an air of sentimental regret at its own inconvenient profundity. Many a worthy youth tells us he almost wishes he could believe. He admires, of all things, the 'moral grandeur'—the 'ethical beauty' of many parts of Christianity; he condescends to patronize Jesus Christ, though he believes that the great mass of words and actions by which alone we know anything about him, are sheer fictions or legends; he believes—gratuitously enough in this instance, for he has no ground for it—that Jesus Christ was a very 'great man' wor-thy of comparison at least with Mahomet, Luther, Napoleon, and 'other heroes'; he even admits that happiness of a simple, child-like faith, in the puerilities of Christianity—it produces such content of mind! But alas! he cannot believe—his intellect is not satisfied—he has revolved the matter too profoundly to be thus taken in; he must, he supposes, (and our beardless philosopher sighs as he says it) bear the penalty of a too restless intellect, and a too speculative genius; he knows all the usual arguments which satisfied Pascal, Butler, Bacon, Leibnitz; but they will do no longer: more radical, more tremendous difficulties have suggested themselves, 'from the 'depths of philosophy,' and far different answers are required now!+

---

* Foxton's last chapter, passim, from some expressions one would almost imagine that our author himself aspired to be, if not the

Messiah, at least the Elias, of this new dispensation. We fear, however, that this 'vox clamantis' would reverse the Baptist's proclamation, and would cry, 'The straight shall be made crooked. and the plain places rough.' + We fear that many young minds in our day are exposed to the danger of falling into one or other of the prevailing forms of unbelief, and especially into that of pantheistic mysticism—from rashly meditating in the cloudy regions of German philosophy—on difficulties which would seem beyond the limits of human reason, but which that philosophy too often promises to solve—with what success we may see from the rapid succession and impenetrable obscurities of its various systems. Alas! when will men learn that one of the highest achievements of philosophy is to know when it is vain to philosophise. When the obscure principles of these most uncouth philosophies, expressed, we verily believe, in the darkest language ever used by civilised man, are applied to the solution of the problems of theology and ethics, no wonder that the natural consequence, as well as just retribution, of such temerity is a plunge into tenfold night. Systems of German philosophy may perhaps be advantageously studied by those who are mature enough to study them; but that they have an incomparable power of intoxicating the intellect of the young aspirant to their mysteries, is, we think, undeniable. They are producing the effect just now in a multitude of our juveniles, who are beclouding themselves in the vain attempt to comprehend ill-translated fragments of ill-understood philosophies, (executed in a sort of Anglicised-German, or Germanised-English, we know not which to call it, but certainly neither German nor English,) from the perusal of which they carry away nothing but some very obscure terms, on which they themselves have superinduced a very vague meaning. These terms you in vain implore them to define; or, if they define them, they define them in terms which as much need definition. Heartily do we wish that Socrates would reappear amongst us, to exercise his accoucheur's art on these hapless Theaetetuses and Menos of our day! Many such youths might no doubt reply at first to the sarcastic Querist, (who might gently complain of a slight cloudiness in their speculations.) that the truths they uttered were too profound for ordinary reasoners. We may easily imagine how Socrates would have dealt with such assumptions. His reply would be rather more severe than that of Mackintosh to Coleridge in a somewhat similar case; namely, that if a notion cannot be made clear to persons who have spent the better part of their days in resolving the difficulties of metaphysics and philosophy, and who are conscious that they are not destitute of patience for the effort requisite to understand them, it may suggest a doubt whether the truth be not in the medium of communication rather than elsewhere; and, indeed, whether the philosopher be not aiming to communicate thoughts on subjects on which man can have no thoughts to communicate. Socrates would add, perhaps, that language was given us to express, not to conceal our thoughts; and that, if they cannot be communicated, invaluable as they doubtless are, we had better keep them to ourselves; one thing it is clear he would do,—he would insist on precise defintions. But in truth it may be more than surmised that the obscurities of which all complain, except those (and in our day they are not a few) to whom obscurity is a recommendation, result from suffering the intellect to speculate in realms forbidden to its access; into caverns of tremendous depth and darkness, with nothing better than our own rushlight. Surely we have reason to suspect as much when some learned professor, after muttering his logical incantations, and conjuring with his logical formulae, surprises you by saying, that he has disposed of the great mysteries of existence and the universe, and solved to your entire satisfaction, in his own curt way, the problems of the ABSOLUTE and the INFINITE! If the cardinal truths of philosophy and religion hitherto received are doomed to be imperilled by such speculations, one feels strongly inclined to pray with the old Homeric hero,—'that if they must perish, it may be at least in daylight.' We earnestly counsel the youthful reader to defer the study of German philosophy, at least till he has matured and disciplined his mind, and familiarised himself with the best models of what used to be our boast—English clearness of thought and expression. He will then learn to ask rigidly for definitions, and not rest satisfied with half-meanings—or no meaning. To the naturally venturous pertinacity of young metaphysicians, few would be disposed to be more indulgent than ourselves. From the time of Plato downwards—who tells us that no sooner do they 'taste' of dialectics than they are ready to dispute with every body—'sparing neither father nor mother, scarcely even the lower animals,' if they had but a voice to reply. They have always expected more from metaphysics than (except as a discipline) they will ever yield. He elsewhere, still more humorously describes the same trait. He compares then, to young dogs who are perpetually snapping at every thing about them:—Hoimai gar se ou lelêthenai, hoti hoi meirakiskoi, hotan to prôton logôn geuôntai, ôs paidia autois katachrôntai, aei eis antilogian chrômenoi kai mimoumenoi tous exelenchontas autoi allous elenchousi, chairontes ôsper skulakia te kai sparattein tous plêsion aei. But we hope we shall not see our metaphysical 'puppies' amusing themselves—as so many 'old dogs' amongst neighbours (who ought to have known better) have done,—by tearing into tatters the sacred leaves of that volume, which contains what is better than all their philosophy.

———

This is easily said, and we know is often said, and loudly. But the justice with which it is said is another matter; for when we can get these cloudy objectors to put down, not their vague assertions of profound difficulties, uttered in the obscure language they love, but a precise statement of their objections, we find them either the very same with those which were quite as powerfully urged in the course of the deistical controversies of the last century (the case with far the greater part), or else such as are of similar character, and susceptible of similar answers. We say not that the answers were always satisfactory, nor are now inquiring whether any of them were so; we merely maintain that the objections in question are not the novelties they affect to be. We say this to obviate an advantage which the very vagueness of much modern opposition to Christianity would obtain, from the notion that some prodigious arguments have been discovered which the intellect of a Pascal or a Butler was not comprehensive enough to anticipate, and which no Clarke or Paley would have been logician enough to refute. We affirm, without hesitation, that when the new advocates of infidelity descend from their airy elevation, and state their objections in intelligible terms, they are found, for the most part, what we have represented them. When we read many of the speculations of German infidelity, we seem to be re-perusing many of our own authors of the last century. It is as if our neighbours had imported our manufactures; and, after re-packing them, in new forms and with some additions, had re-shipped and sent them back to us as new commodities. Hardly an instance of discrepancy is mentioned in the 'Wolfenbutted Fragments,' which will not be found in the pages of our own deists a century ago; and, as already hinted, of Dr. Strauss's elaborate strictures, the vast majority will be found in the same sources. In fact, though far from thinking it to our national credit, none but those who will dive a little deeper than most do into a happily forgotten portion of our literature, (which made noise enough in its day, and created very superfluous terrors for the fate of Christianity,) can have any idea of the extent to which the modern forms of unbelief in Germany—so far as founded on any positive grounds, whether of reason or of criticism,—are indebted to our English Deists. Tholuck, however, and others of his countrymen, seem thoroughly aware of it.

The objections to the truth of Christianity are directed either against the evidence itself; or that which it substantiates. Against the latter, as Bishop Butler says, unless the objections be truly such as prove contradictions in it, they are 'perfectly frivolous;' since we cannot be competent judges either as to what it is worthy of the Supreme Mind to reveal, or how far a portion of an imperfectly-developed system may harmonise with the whole; and, perhaps, on many points, we never can be competent judges, unless we can cease to be finite. The objections to the evidence itself are, as the same great author observes, 'well worthy of the fullest attention.' The a priori objection to miracles we have already briefly touched. If that objection be valid, it is vain to argue further; but if not, the remaining objections must be powerful enough to neutralise the entire mass of the evidence, and, in fact, to mount to a proof of contradictions; 'not on this or that minute point of historic detail,—but on such as shake the foundations of the whole edifice of evidence. It will not do to say, 'Here is a minute discrepancy in the history of Matthew or Luke as compared with that of 'Mark or John;' for, first, such discrepancies are often found, in other authors, to be apparent, and not real,—founded on our taking for granted that there is no circumstance unmentioned by two writers which, if known, would have been seen to harmonise their statements. We admit this possible reconciliation readily enough in the case of many seeming discrepancies of other historians; but it is a benefit which men are slow to admit in the case of the sacred narratives. There the objector is always apt to take it for granted that the discrepancy is real; though it may be easy to suppose a case (a possible case is quite sufficient for the purpose) which would neutralise the objection. Of this perverseness (we can call it by no other name) the examples are perpetual in the critical tortures which Strauss has subjected the sacred historians.*"—

It may be objected, perhaps, that the gratuitous supposition of some unmentioned fact—which, if mentioned, would harmonise the apparently counter-statements of two historians—cannot be admitted, and is, in fact, a surrender of the argument. But to say so, is only to betray an utter ignorance of what the argument is. If an objection be founded on the alleged absolute contradiction of two statements, it is quite sufficient to show any (not the real, but only a hypothetical and possible) medium of reconciling them; and the objection is, in all fairness, dissolved. And this would be felt by the honest logician, even if we did not know of any such instances in point of fact. We do know however, of many. Nothing is more common than to find, in the narration of two perfectly honest historians,—referring to the same events from different points of view, or for a different purpose,—the omission a fact which gives a seeming contrariety to their statements; a contrariety which the mention of the omitted fact by a third writer instantly clears up.+

----

* The reader may see some striking instances of his disposition to take the worse sense, in Beard's 'Voices of the Church.' Tholuck truly observes, too, in his strictures on Strauss, 'We know how frequently the loss of a few words in one ancient author would be sufficient to cast an inexplicable obscurity over another.' The same writer well observes, that there never was a historian who, if treated on the principles of criticism which his countryman has applied to the Evangelists, might not be proved a mere mytholographer ... 'It is plain', he says, 'that if absolute among historians'—and still more absolute apparent agreement—is necessary to assure us that we possess in their writings credible history, we must renounce all pretence to any such possession.' The translations from Quinet, Coquerel, and Tholuck are all, in different ways, well worth read-

ing. The last truly says, 'Strauss came to the study of the Evangelical history with the forgone conclusion that "miracles are impossible;" and where an investigator brings with him an absolute conviction of the guilt of the accused to the examination of his case, we know how even the most innocent may be implicated and condemned out of his own mouth.' In fact, so strong and various are the proofs of truth and reality in the history of the New Testament, that none would ever have suspected the veracity of the writers, or tried to disprove it, except for the above forgone conclusion—'that miracles are impossible.' We also recommend to the reader an ingenious brochure included in the 'Voices of the Church, in reply to Strauss,' constructed on the same principle with Whately's admirable 'Historic Doubts,' namely; 'The Fallacy of the Mythical Theory of Dr. Strauss, illustrated from the History of Martin Luther, and from the actual Mohammedan Myths of the Life of Jesus.' What a subject for the same play of ingenuity would be Dean Swift! The date, and place of his birth disputed—whether he was an Englishman or an Irishman—his incomprehensible relations to Stella and Vanessa, utterly incomprehensible on any hypothesis—his alleged seduction of one of one, of both, of neither—his marriage with Stella affirmed, disputed, and still wholly unsettled—the numberless other incidents in his life full of contradiction and mystery—and, not least, the eccentricities and inconsistencies of his whole character and conduct! Why, with a thousandth part of Dr. Strauss's assumptions, it would be easy to reduce Swift to as fabulous a personage as his own Lemuel Gulliver. +Any apparent discrepancy with either themselves or profane historians is usually sufficient to satisfy Dr. Strauss. He is ever ready to conclude that the discrepancy is real, and that the profane historians are right. In adducing some striking instances of the minute accuracy of Luke, only revealed by obscure collateral evidence (historic or numismatic) discovered since, Tholuck remarks, 'What an outcry would have been made had not the specious appearance of error been thus obviated. Luke calls Gallio proconsul of Achaia: we should not have expected it, since though Achaia was originally to senatorial province. Tiberius had changed it into an imperial one, and the title of its governor, therefore, was procurator; now a passage in Suetonius informs us, that Claudius had restored the province to the senate.' The same Evangelist calls Sergius Paulus governor of Cyprus; yet we might have expected to find only a praetor, since Cyprus was an imperial province. In this case, again: says Tholuck, the correctness of the historian has been remarkable attested. Coins and later still a passage in Dion Cassius, have been found, giving proof that Augustus restored the province to the senate; and thus, as if to vindicate the Evangelist, the Roman historian adds, 'Thus, proconsuls began to be sent into that island also.' Trans. From Tholuck, pp. 21, 22. In the same manner coins have been found proving he is correct in some other once disputed instances. Is it not fair to suppose that many apparent discrepancies of the same order may be eventually removed by similar evidence?

———

Very forgetful of this have the advocates of infidelity usually been: nay, (as if they would make up in the number of objections what they want in weight,) they have frequently availed themselves not only of apparent contrarieties, but of mere incompleteness in the statements of two different writers, on which to found a charge of contradiction. Thus, if one writer says that a certain person was present at a given time or place, when another says that he and two more were there; or that one man was cured of blindness, when another says that two were, — such a thing is often alleged as a contradiction; whereas, in truth, it resents not even a difficulty — unless one historian be bound to say not only all that another says but just so much, and no more. Let such objections be what they will, unless they prove absolute contradictions in the narrative, they are as mere dust in the balance, compared with the stupendous mass and variety of that evidence which confirms the substantial truth of Christianity. And even if they establish real contradictions, they still amount, for reasons we are about to state, to dust in the balance, unless they establish contradictions not in immaterial but in vital points. The objections must be such as, if proved, leave the whole fabric of evidence in ruins. For, secondly, we are fully disposed to concede to the objector that there are, in the books of Scripture, not only apparent but real discrepancies, — a point which many of the advocates of Christianity are, indeed, reluctant to admit but which we think, no candid advocate will feel to be the less true. Nevertheless, even such an advocate of the Scriptures may justly contend that the very reasons which necessitate this admission of discrepancies also reduce them to such a limit that they do not affect, in the slightest degree, the substantial credibility of the sacred records; and, in our judgment, Christians have unwisely damaged their cause, and given a needless advantage to the infidel, by denying that any discrepancies exist, or by endeavouring to prove that they do not. The discrepancies to which we refer are just those which, in the course of the transcription of ancient books, divine or human, through many ages,—their constant transcription by different hands,—their translation into various languages,—may not only be expected to occur, but which must occur, unless there be a perpetual series of most minute and ludicrous miracles—certainly never promised, and as certainly never performed—to counteract all the effects of negligence and inadvertence, to guide the pen of every transcriber to infallible accuracy, and to prevent his ever deviating into any casual error! Such miraculous intervention, we need not say, has never been pleaded for by any apologist of Christianity; has certainly never been promised; and, if it had,—since we see, as a matter of fact, that the promise has never been fulfilled,—the whole of Christianity would fall to the ground. But then, from a large induction, we know that the limits within which discrepancies and errors from such causes will occur, must be very moderate; we know, from numberless examples of other writings, what the maximum is,—and that it leaves their substantial authenticity untouched and unimpeached. No one supposes the writings of Plato and Cicero, of Thucydides and Tacitus, of Bacon or Shakspeare, fundamentally vitiated by the like discrepancies, errors, and absurdities which time and inadvertence have occasioned.

The corruptions in the Scriptures from these causes are likely to be even less than in the case of any other writings; from their very structure,—the varied and reiterated forms in which all the great truths are expressed; from the greater veneration they inspired; the greater care with which they would be transcribed; the greater number of copies which would be diffused through the world,— and which, though that very circumstance would multiply the number of variations, would also afford, in their collation, the means of reciprocal correction;—a correction which we have seen applied in our day, with admirable success, to so many ancient writers, under a system of canons which have now raised this species of criticism to the rank of an inductive science. This criticism, applied to the Scriptures, has in many instances restored the true rending, and dissolved the objections which might have been founded on the uncorrected variations; and, as time rolls on, may lead, by yet fresh discoveries and more comprehensive recensions, to a yet further clarifying of the stream of Divine truth, till 'the river of the water of life' shall flow nearly in its original limpid purity. Within such limits as these, the most consistent advocate of Christianity not only must admit — not only may safely admit — the existence of discrepancies, but may do so even with advantage to his cause. he must admit them, since such variations must be the result of the manner in which the records have been transmitted, unless we suppose a supernatural intervention, neither promised by God nor pleaded for by man: he may safely admit them, because — from a general induction from the history of all literature — we see that, where copies of writings have been sufficiently multiplied, and sufficient motives for care have existed in the transcription, the limits of error are very narrow, and leave the substantial identity untouched: and he may admit them with advantage; for the admission is a reply to many objections rounded on the assumption that he must contend that there are no variations, when he need only contend that there are none that can be material.

But it may be said, 'May not we be permitted, while conceding the miraculous and other evidences of Christianity, and the general authority of the records which contain it, to go a step further, and to reject some things which seem palpably ill-reasoned, distasteful, inconsistent, or immoral?' 'Let every man be fully persuaded in his own mind.' For ourselves, we honestly confess we cannot see the logical consistency of such a position; any more than the reasonableness, after having admitted the preponderant evidence for the great truth of Theism, of excepting some phenomena as apparently at variance with the Divine perfections; and thus virtually adopting a Manichaean hypothesis. We must recollect that we know nothing of Christianity except from its records; and as these, once fairly ascertained to be authentic and genuine, are all, as regards their contents, supported precisely by the same miraculous and other evidence; as they bear upon them precisely the same internal marks of artlessness, truth, and sincerity; and, historically and in other respects, are inextricably interwoven with one another; we see not on what principles we can safely reject portions as improbable, distasteful, not quadrating with the dictates of reason;' our 'intuitional consciousness,' and what not. This assumed liberty, however is, as we apprehend, of the very essence of Rationalism; and it may be called the Manichaeism of interpretation. So long as the canonicity of any of the records, or any portion of them, or their true interpretation, is in dispute, we may fairly doubt; but that point once decided by honest criticism, to say we receive such and such portions, on account of the weight of the general evidence, and yet reject other portions, though sustained by the same evidence, because we think there is something unreasonable or revolting in their substance, is plainly to accept evidence only where it pleases us, and to reject it where it pleases us not. The only question fairly at issue must ever be whether the general evidence for Christianity will overbear the difficulty which we cannot separate from the truths. If it will not, we must reject it wholly; and if it will, we must receive it wholly. There is plainly no tenable position between absolute infidelity and absolute belief. And this is proved by the infinitely various and Protean character of Rationalism, and the perfectly indeterminate, but always arbitrary, limits it imposes on itself. It exists in all forms and degrees, from a moderation which accepts nearly the entire system of Christianity, and which certainly rejects nothing that can be said to constitute its distinctive truth, to an audacity of unbelief, which, professing still vaguely to reverence Christianity as 'something divine,' sponges out nine tenths of the whole; or, after reducing the mass of it to a caput mortuum of lies, fiction, and superstitions, retains only a few drops of fact and doctrine, — so few as certainly not to pay for the expenses of the critical distillation.*

———

* It may be as well to remark, that we have frequently observed a disposition to represent the very general abandonment of the theory of 'verbal inspiration' as a concession to Rationalism; as if it necessarily followed from admitting that inspiration is not verbal, that therefore an indeterminate portion of the substance or doctrine is purely human. It is plain, however, that this is no necessary consequence: an advocate of plenary inspiration may contend, that,

though he does not believe that the very words of Scripture were dictated, yet that the thoughts were either so suggested, (if the matter was such as could be known only by revelation,) or so controlled, (if the matter were such as was previously known,) that (excluding errors introduced into the text since) the Scriptures as first composed were—what no book of man ever was, or can be, even in the plainest narrative of the simplest events—a perfectly accurate expression of truth. We enter not here, however, into the question whether such a view of inspiration is better or worse than another. We are simply anxious to correct a fallacy which has, judging from what we have recently read, operated rather extensively. Inspiration may be verbal, or the contrary; but, whether one or the other, he who takes the affirmative or negative of that question may still consistently contend that it may still be plenary. The question of the inspiration of the whole or the inspiration of a part, is widely different from that as to the suggestion of the words or the suggestion of the thoughts. But these questions we leave to professed theologians. We merely enter our protest against a prevailing fallacy.

———

Nor will the theory of what some call the 'intuitional consciousness avail us here. It is true, as they assert, that the constitution of human nature is such that, before its actual development, it has a capacity of developing to certain effects only,—just as the flower in the germ, as it expands to the sun, will have certain colours and a certain fragrance, and no other;—all which, indeed, though not very new or profound, is very important. But it is not so dear that it will give us any help on the present occasion. We have an original susceptibility of music, of beauty, of religion, it is said. Granted; but as the actual development of this susceptibility exhibits all the diversities between Handel's notions of harmony and those of an American Indian—between Raphael's notions of beauty and those of a Hottentot—between St. Paul's notions of a God and those of a New Zealander—it would appear that the education of this susceptibility is at least as important as the susceptibility itself, if not more so; for without the susceptibility itself, we should simply have no notion of music, beauty, or religion; and between such negation and that notion of all these which New Zealanders and Hottentots possess, not a few of our species would probably prefer the former. It is in vain then to tell us to look into the 'depths of our own nature' (as some vaguely say), and to judge thence what, in a professed revelation, is suitable to us, or worthy of our acceptance and rejection respectively. This criterion is, as we see by the utterly different judgments formed by different classes of Rationalists as to the how much they shall receive of the revelation they might generally admit, a very shifting one — a measure which has no linear unit; it is to employ, as mathematicians say, a variable as if it were a constant quantity; or, rather, it is to attempt to find the value of an unknown quantity by another equally unknown.

We cannot but judge, then, the principles of Rationalism to be logically untenable. And we do so, not merely or principally on account of the absurdity it involves, — that God has expressly supplemented human reason by a revelation containing an indeterminate but large portion of falsities, errors, and absurdities and which we are to commit to our little alembic, and distil as we may; not only from the absurdity of supposing that God has demanded our faith, for statements which are to be received only as they appear perfectly comprehensible by our reason; — or, in other words, only for what it is impossible that we should doubt or deny; not merely because the principle inevitably leaves man to construct the so-called revelation entirely for himself; so that what one man receives as genuine communication from heaven, another, from having a different development of 'his intuitional consciousness,' rejects as an absurdity too gross for human belief: — Not wholly, we say, nor even principally, for these reasons; but for the still stronger reason, that such a system of objections is an egregious trifling with that great complex mass of evidence which, as we have said, applies to the whole of Christianity or to none of it. As if to baffle the efforts of man consistently to disengage these elements of our belief, the whole are inextricably blended together. The supernatural element, especially, is so diffused through all the records, that it is more and more felt, at every step, to be impossible to obliterate it without obliterating the entire system in which it circulates. The stain, if stain it be, is far too deep for any scouring fluids of Rationalism to wash it out, without destroying the whole texture of our creed: and, in our judgment, the only consistent Rationalism is the Rationalism which rejects it all.

At whatever point the Rationalist we have attempted to describe may take his stand, we do not think it difficult to prove that his conduct is eminently irrational. If, for example, he be one of those moderate Rationalists who admit (as thousands do) the miraculous and other evidence of the supernatural origin of the Gospel, and therefore also admit such and such doctrines to be true,—what can he reply, if further asked what reason he can have for accepting these truths and rejecting others which are supported by the very same evidence? How can he be sure that the truths he receives are established by evidence which, to all appearance, equally authenticates the falsehoods he rejects? Surely, as already said, this is to reject and accept evidence as he pleases. If, on the other hand, he says that he receives the miracles only to authenticate what he knows very well without them, and believes true on the information of reason alone, why trouble miracles and revelation at all? Is not this, according to the old proverb to 'take a hatchet to break an egg'?*

———

* If such a man says that he rejects certain doctrines, not on rationalistic grounds, but because he denies the canonical authority, or the interpretation of portions of the records in which they are found, and is willing to abide by the issue if the evidence on those points—evidence with which the human mind is quite competent to deal,—we answer, that he is not the man with whom we are now arguing. The points in dispute will be determined by the honest use of history, criticism, and philology. But between such a man and one who rejects Christianity altogether, we can imagine no consistent position.

———

Nor can we disguise from ourselves, indeed, that consistency in the application of the essential principle of Rationalism would compel us to go a few steps further; for since, as Bishop Butler has shown, no greater difficulties (if so great) attach to the page of Revelation than to the volume of Nature itself,—especially those which are involved in that dread enigma, 'the origin of evil,' compared with which all other enigmas are trifles,—that abyss into which so many of the difficulties of all theology, natural and revealed, at last disembogue themselves,—we feel that the admission of the principle of Rationalism would ultimately drive us, not only to reject Christianity, but to reject Theism in all its forms, whether Monotheism, or Pantheism, and even positive or dogmatic Atheism itself. Nor could we stop, indeed, till we had arrived at that absolute pyrrhonism which consists, if such a thing be possible, in the negation of all belief,—even to the belief that we do not believe!

But though the objections to the reception of Christianity are numerous, and some insoluble, the question always returns, whether they over balance the mass of the evidence in its favour? nor is it to be forgotten that they are susceptible of indefinite alleviation as time rolls on; and with a few observations on this point we will close the present article.

A refinement of modern philosophy often leads our rationalist to speak depreciatingly, if not contemptuously, of what he calls a stereotyped revelation—revelation in a book. It ties down, he is fond of saying, the spirit to the letter; and limits the 'progress' and 'development' of the human mind in its 'free' pursuit of truth. The answer we should be disposed to make is, first, that if a book does contain truth, the sooner that truth is stereotyped the better; secondly, that if such book, like the book of Nature, or, as we deem, the book of Revelation, really contains truth, its study, so far from being incompatible with the spirit of free inquiry, will invite and repay continual efforts more completely to understand it. Though the great and fundamental truths contained in either volume will be obvious in proportion to their importance and necessity, there is no limit to be placed on the degree of accuracy with which the truths they severally contain may be deciphered, stated, adjusted—or even on the period in which fragments of new truth shall cease to be elicited. It is true indeed that theology cannot be said to admit of unlimited progress, in the same sense as chemistry—which may, for aught we know, treble or quadruple its present accumulations, vast as they are, both in bulk and importance. But, even in theology as deduced from the Scripture, minute fragments of new truth, or more exact adjustments of old truth, may be perpetually expected. Lastly, we shall reply, that the objection to a revelation's being consigned to a 'book' is singularly inapposite, considering that by the constitution of the world and of human nature, man, without books,—without the power of recording, transmitting, and perpetuating thought, of rendering it permanent and diffusive, ever is, ever has been, and ever must be little better than a savage; and therefore, if there was to be a revelation at all, it might fairly be expected that it would be communicated in this form; thus affording us one more analogy, in addition to the many which Butler has stated, and which may in time be multiplied without end, between 'Revealed Religion and the Constitution and Course of Nature.'

And this leads us to notice a saying of that comprehensive genius, which we do not recollect having seen quoted in connexion with recent controversies, but which is well worthy of being borne in mind, as teaching us to beware of hastily assuming that objections to Revelation, whether suggested by the progress of science, or from the supposed incongruity of its own contents, are unanswerable. We are not, he says, rashly to suppose that we have arrived at the true meaning of the whole of that book. 'It is not at all incredible that a book which has been so long in the possession of mankind, should contain many truths as yet undiscerned. For all the same phenomena and the same faculties of investigation, from which such great discoveries in natural knowledge have been made in the present and last age, were equally in the possession of mankind several thousand year's before.' These words are worthy of Butler: and as many illustrations of their truth have been supplied since his day, so many others may fairly be anticipated in the course of time. Several distinct species of argument for the truth of Christianity from the very structure and contents of the books containing it have been invented—of which Paley's 'Horae Paulinae' is a memorable example. The diligent collation of the text, too, has removed many difficulties; the diligent study of the original languages of ancient history, manners and customs, has cleared up many more; and by supplying proof of accuracy where error of falsehood had been charged, has supplied important additions to the evidence which substantiates the truth of Revelation. Against the alleged absurdity of the laws of Moses, again, such works as that of Micholis have disclosed much of that relative wisdom which aims not at the abstractedly best, but the best which a given condition of humanity, a given period of the world's history, and a given purpose could dictate. In pondering such difficulties as still remain in those laws, we may remember the answer of Solon to the question, whether he had given the Athenians the best laws; viz. that he had given them the best of which they were capable: or the judgment of the illustrious Montesquieu, who remarks, 'When Divine Wisdom said to the Jews, "I have given you precepts which are not good," this signifies that they had only a relative goodness: and this is the sponge which wipes out all the difficulties which are to be found in the laws of Moses.' This is a truth which we are persuaded a profound philosophy will understand the better the more deeply it is revolved; and only those legislative pedants will refuse weight to it, who would venturously propose to give New Zealanders and Hottentots, in the starkness of their savage ignorance, the complex forms of the British constitution. In similar manner, many of the old objections of our deistical writers have ceased to be heard of in our day, unless it be from the lips of the veriest sciolism; the objections, for instance, of that truly pedantic philosophy which once argued that ethical and religious truth are not given in the Scripture in a system such as a schoolman might have digested it into; as if the brief iteration and varied illustration of pregnant truth, intermingled with narrative, parable, and example, were not infinitely better adapted to the condition of the human intellect in general! For similar reasons, the old objection, that statements of Christian morality are given without the requisite limitations, and cannot be literally acted upon, has been long since abandoned as an absurdity. It is granted that a hundred folios could not contain the hundredth part of all the limitations of human actions, and all the possible cases of a contentious casuistry; and it is also granted that human nature is not so inept as to be incapable of interpreting and limiting for itself such rules as 'Whatsoever ye would that men should do to you, do ye even so to them.'

In the same manner have many of the objections suggested at different periods by the progress of science been dissolved; and, amongst the rest, those alleged from the remote historic antiquity of certain nations on which infidels, like Volney and Voltaire, once so confidently relied. And it is worthy of remark, that some of the old objections of philosophers have disappeared by the aid of that very science—geology—which has led, as every new branch of science probably will, to new ones. Geology has, however, in our judgment, done at least as much already to remove difficulties as to occasion them; and it is not illogical, or perhaps unfair, to surmise that, we will only have patience, its own difficulties, as those of so many other branches of science, will be eventually solved. One thing is clear,—that, if the Bible be true and geology be true, that cannot be geologically true which is scripturally false, or vice versa; and we may therefore laugh at the polite compromise which is sometimes affected by learned professors of theology and geology respectively. All we demand of either—all that is needed—is, that they refrain from a too hasty conclusion of absolute contradictions between their respective sciences, and retain quiet remembrance of the imperfection of our present knowledge both of geology and, as Butler says, of the Bible. The recent interpretation of the commencement of Genesis—by which the first verse is simply supposed to affirm the original creation of all things, while the second immediately refers to the commencement of the human economy; passing by those prodigious cycles which geology demands, with a silence worthy of a true revelation, which does not pretend to gratify our curiosity as to the previous condition of our globe any more than our curiosity as to the history of other worlds—was first suggested by geology, though suspected and indeed anticipated by some of the early church Fathers. But it is now felt by multitudes to be the more reasonable interpretation,—the second verse certainly more naturally suggesting previous revolutions in the history of the earth than its then instant creation: and though we frankly concede that we have not yet seen any account of the whole first chapter of Genesis which quadrates with the doctrines of geology, it does not become us hastily to conclude that there can be none. If a further adjustment of those doctrines, and a more diligent investigation of the Scripture together, should hereafter suggest any possible harmony,—though not the true one but one ever so gratuitously assumed,—it will be sufficient to neutralise the objection. This, it will be observed, is in accordance with what has been already shown,—that wherever an objection is founded on an apparent contradiction between two statements, it is sufficient to show any possible way in which the statements may be reconciled, whether the true one or not. The objection, in that case, to the supposition that the facts are gratuitously assumed, though often urged, is, in reality, nothing to the purpose.* If it should ever be shown, for example, that supposing as many geological eras as the philosopher requires to have passed in the chasm between the first verse, which asserts the original dependence of all things on the fiat of the Creator, and the second, which is supposed to commence the human era, any imaginable condition of our system — at the close, so to speak, of a given geological period — would harmonise with a fair interpretation of the first chapter or Genesis, the objection will be neutralised.

----

* Some admirable remarks in relation to the answers we are bound to give to objections to revealed religion have been made by Leibnitz (in reply to Bayle) in the little tract prefixed to his Theodicee, entitled 'De la Conformite de la Foi avec la Raison.' He there shows that the utmost that can fairly be asked is, to prove that the affirmed truths involve no necessary contradiction.

----

We have little doubt in our own minds that the ultimately converging though, it may be, transiently discrepant conclusions of the sciences of philology, ethnology, and geology (in all of which we may rest assured great discoveries are yet to be made) will tend to harmonise with the ultimate results of a more thorough study of the records of the race as contained in the book of Revelation. Let us be permitted to imagine one example of such possible harmony. We think that the philologist may engage to make out, on the strictest principles of induction, from the tenacity with which all communities cling to their language, and the slow observed rate of change by which they alter; by which Anglo-Saxon, for example has become English*, Latin Italian, and ancient Greek modern (though these languages have been affected by every conceivable cause of variation and depravation); that it would require hundreds of thousands, nay millions, of years to account for the production, by known natural causes, of the vast multitude of totally distinct languages, and tens of thousands of dialects, which man now utters. On the other hand, the geologist is more and more persuaded of comparatively recent origin of the human race. What, then, is to harmonise these conflicting statements? Will it not be curious if it should turn out that nothing can possibly harmonise them but the statement of Genesis, that in order to prevent the natural tendency of the race to accumulate on one spot and facilitate their dispersion and destined occupancy of the globe, a preternatural intervention expedited the operation of the causes which would gradually have given birth to distinct languages? Of the probability of this intervention, some profound philologist have, on scientific grounds alone, expressed their conviction. But in all such matters, what we plead for is only — patience; we wish not to dogmatise; all we ask is, a philosophic abstinence from dogmatism. In relation to many difficulties, what is now a reasonable exercise of faith may one day be rewarded by a knowledge which on those particular points may terminate it. And, in such ways, it is surely conceivable that a great part of the objections against Revelation may, in time, disappear; and, though other objections may be the result of the progress of the other sciences or the origination of new, the solution of previous objections, together with the additions to the evidences of Christianity, external and internal, which the study of history and of the Scriptures may supply, and the still brighter light cast by the progress of Christianity and the fulfilment of its prophecies, may inspire increasing confidence that the new objections are also destined to yield to similar solvents. Meanwhile, such new difficulties, and those more awful and gigantic shadows which we have no reason to believe will ever be chased from the sacred page, — mysteries which probably could not be explained from the necessary limitation of our faculties, and are, at all events, submitted to us as a salutary discipline of our humility, — will continue to form that exercise of faith which is probably nearly equal in every age — and necessary in all ages, if we would be made 'little children,' qualified 'to enter the kingdom of God.'

————

+ It contains, let us recollect, (after all causes of changes, including a conquest, have been at work upon it,) a vast majority of the Saxon words spoken in the time of Alfred—nearly a thousand years ago!

———

In conclusion we may remark, that while many are proclaiming that Christianity is effete, and that, in the language of Mr. Proudhon (who complacently says it amidst the ignominious failure of a thousand social panaceas or his own age and country), it will certainly 'die out in about three hundred years;' and while many more proclaim that, as a religion of supernatural origin and supernatural evidence, it is already dying, if not dead; we must beg leave to remind them that, even if 'Christianity be false, as they allege, they are utterly forgetting the maxims of a cautious induction in saying that it will therefore cease to exert dominion over mankind. What proof is there of this? Whether true or false, it has already survived numberless revolutions of human opinions, and all sorts of changes and assaults. It is not confined, like other religions, to any one race—to any one clime—or any one form of political constitution. While it transmigrates freely from race to race, and clime to clime, its chief home; too, is still in the bosom of enterprise, wealth, science, and civilisation; and it is at this moment most powerful amongst the nations that have most of these. If not true, it has such an appearance of truth as to have satisfied many of the acutest and most powerful intellects of the species;—a Bacon, a Pascal, a Leibnitz, a Locke, a Newton, a Butler;—such an appearance of truth as to have enlisted in its support an immense army of genius and learning: genius and learning, not only in some sense professional, and often wrongfully represented as therefore interested, but much of both, strictly extra-professional; animated to its defence by nothing but a conviction of the force of the arguments by which its truth is sustained, and that 'hope full of immortality' which its promises have inspired. Under such circumstances it must appear equally rash and gratuitous to suppose, even if it be a delusion, that an institute, which has thus enlisted the sympathies of so many of the greatest minds of all races and of all ages—which is alone stable and progressive amidst instability and fluctuation, — will soon come to an end. Still more absurdly premature is it to raise a paean over its fall, upon every new attack upon it, when it has already survived so many. This, in fact, is a tone which, though every age renews it, should long since have been rebuked by the constant falsification of similar prophecies, from the time of Julian to the time of Bolingbroke, and from the time of Bolingbroke to the time of Strauss. As Addison, we think, humorously tells the Atheist, that he is hasty in his logic when he infers that if there be no God, immortality must be a delusion, since, if chance has actually found him a place in this bad world, it may, perchance, hereafter find him another place in a worse, — -so we say, that if Christianity be a delusion, since it is a delusion which has been proof against so much of bitter opposition, and has imposed upon such hosts of mighty intellects, these is nothing to show that it will not do so still, in spite of the efforts either of Proudhon or a Strauss. Such a tone was, perhaps, never so triumphant as during the heat of the Deistical controversy in our own country, and to which Butler alludes with so much characteristic but deeply satirical simplicity, in the preface to his great work: — 'It is come,' says he, 'I know not how, to be taken for granted by many persons that Christianity is not so much a subject of inquiry, but that it is now at length discovered to be fictitious …. On the contrary, thus much at least will here be found, not taken for granted, but proved, that any reasonable man, who will thoroughly consider the matter, may be as much assured as he is of his own being, that it is not, however, so clear that there is nothing in it.' The Christian, we conceive, may now say the same to the Froudes, and Foxtons, and to much more formidable adversaries of the present day. Christianity, we doubt not, will still live, when they and their works, and the refutations of their works, are alike forgotten; and a new series of attacks and defences shall have occupied for a while (as so many others have done) the attention of the world. Christianity, like Rome, has had both the Gaul and Hannibal at her gates: But as the 'Eternal City' in the latter case calmly offered for sale, and sold, at an undepreciated price, the very ground on which the Carthaginian had fixed his camp, with equal calmness may Christianity imitate her example of magnanimity. She may feel assured that, as in so many past instances of premature triumph on the part of her enemies, the ground they occupy will one day be its own; that the very discoveries, apparently hostile, of science and philosophy, will be a great extent with the discoveries in chronology and history; and thus will it be, we are confident, (and to a certain extent has been already), with those in geology. That science has done much, not only to render the old theories of Atheism untenable and to familiarise the minds of men to the idea of miracles, by that of successive creations, but to confirm the Scriptural statement of the comparatively recent origin of our Race. Only the men of science and the men of theology must alike Guard against the besetting fallacy of their kind,—that of too hastily taking for granted that they already know the whole of their respective sciences, and of forgetting the declaration of the Apostle, equally true of all man's attainments, whether in one department of science or another,—'We know but in part, and we prophesy in part.'

Though Socrates perhaps expressed himself too absolutely when he said that 'he only knew nothing,' yet a tinge of the same spirit,—a deep conviction of the profound ignorance of the human mind, even at its best—has ever been a characteristic of the most comprehensive genius. It has been a topic on which it has been fond of mournfully dilating. It is thus with Socrates, with Plato, with Bacon (even amidst all his magnificent aspirations and bold predictions), with Newton, with Pascal, and especially with Butler, in whom, if in any, the sentiment is carried to excess. We need not say that it is seldom found in the writings of those modern speculators who rush, in the hardihood of their adventurous logic, on a solution of the problems of the Absolute and the Infinite, and resolve in delightfully brief demonstrations the mightiest problems of the universe—those great enigmas, from which true philosophy shrinks, not because it has never ventured to think of them, but because it has thought of them enough to know that it is in vain to attempt their solution. To know the limits of human philosophy is the 'better part' of all philosophy; and though the conviction of our ignorance is humiliating, it is, like every true conviction, salutary. Amidst this night of the soul, bright stars—far distant fountains of illumination—are wont to steal out, which shine not while the imagined Sun of reason is above the horizon! and it is in that night, as in the darkness of outward nature, that we gain our only true ideas of the illimitable dimensions of the universe, and of our true position in it.

Meanwhile we conclude that God has created 'two great lights,'—
the greater light to rule man's busy day—and that is Reason, and
the lesser to rule his contemplative night—and that is Faith.

But faith itself shines only so long as she reflects some faint
Illumination from the brighter orb.